THE
HONORABLE
OUTSIDERS

(LOS FORASTEROS HONORABLES)

John Higgins

Dear Ed,

Wishing you and your
family all the best for 2021

Jack.

ISBN (Print): 978-1-09831-825-3
ISBN (eBook): 978-1-09831-826-0

Cover Photos:
Casa la Siesta – Pierre Richardson Photography
Spanish rooftops – Russell Witherington
Cover Design by Robert Barthelmes

McDonough
Press

mcdonoughpress@gmail.com
McDonough Press
P.O. Box 54402
Philadelphia, PA 19148

Available on line globally

⁄⁄∣BookBaby

ACKNOWLEDGEMENTS

I could not have written this book without the encouragement of our
Blue-Eyed Irish American Writers group.
We met almost
monthly for many years; the age of the group members
spanned four generations
and seventy-two years.
Even when it was hard for me to believe that I would
actually be able to finish this book, they
encouraged me not to give up.

I also owe a debt of gratitude to Margie Strosser for her editorial
advice, patience, and support
as I wrote and rewrote many parts of this book,
and to the many friends who
read various drafts and provided valuable advice and corrections.

Most of all I want to thank my wife, Raquel Montilla Alcazar, who
has been devoted to her Spanish heritage and my guide to
understanding this remarkable country for
the fifty years of our marriage.

THE HONORABLE OUTSIDERS
(LOS FORASTEROS HONORABLES)
by
John Higgins

In Spain where death is the national spectacle
the dead are more alive than
the dead of any other country in the world.
Their shadow wounds like the edge of a barber's razor.
Frederico Garcia Lorca

Turning and turning in the widening gyre
The falcon cannot hear the falconer;
Things fall apart; the center cannot hold;
Mere anarchy is loosed upon the world,
the blood-dimmed tide is loosed, and everywhere
the ceremony of innocence is drowned.
The best lack all conviction, while the worst
Are full of passionate intensity.
William Butler Yeats

Black are the horses,
The horseshoes are black.
On the dark capes glisten
stains of ink and of wax.
Their skulls are leaden,
which is why they don't weep.
With their patent leather souls
they come down the street.
Federico Garcia Lorca

Edwin Benedict Fitzgerald, twenty-three years old. Born and raised in Dublin, he came to Los Olivares to become the tutor to Luis Eduardo's three children.

Andrew Fitzgerald, Edwin's father, a wealthy cement manufacturer in Dublin.

Luis Eduardo, Third Conde de Villanueva de Granada, forty-one years old, lives at his family's estate, Los Olivares, in the South of Spain.

Katherine Hardgrave, Luis Eduardo's wife, British, thirty-one years old, from a wealthy Yorkshire woolen mills owning family.

Their three children:
> Leander, age nine
> Oscar, age seven
> Ottilie, age four

Don Carlo, 2nd Conde de Villanueva de Granada. Father of Luis Eduardo, lives in Madrid with Begonia, his second wife.

Begonia, Duquesa de Brabant y Burmay and Condesa de Villanueva de Granada, from an impoverished aristocratic family in Murcia.

Augustin Beltran, manager of the farm at Los Olivares.

Manuel de Montilla, the new schoolteacher at Los Olivares.

Guillermo Perez, leader of the local peasants.

GUESTS AT LOS OLIVARES

Don Pedro Segura y Saenz, Cardinal Archbishop at Toledo and Papal Nuncio to Spain, Luis Eduardo's uncle.

Constancia De la Mora, grandaughter of an important prime minister under Alfonso XIII.

Mercedes Sanz-Bachiller, a friend of Katherine.

The focus of this story is *Misiones Pedagogicas* (Teaching Missions), an educational program established in 1931 by the Republican government whose goal was to provide access to general Spanish culture for the poorest villages. Established interests such as the Church, the Guardia Civil, and the landed gentry opposed *Misiones Pedagogicas* because they saw it as supporting political and cultural change.

TABLE OF CONTENTS

CHAPTER ONE

CHAPTER ONE

My Early Life

My name is Edwin Benedict Fitzgerald. My mother died when I was 11 years old. Before that she had been the center of a lively social circle. Her death transformed our household into a silent and unhappy one. No one came to call; window curtains were always drawn; fires were not lit. My father, Andrew Fitzgerald, was devastated by grief. He became a man of severe religious piety, reclusive and depressed.

I had no idea how to express my grief, which was all the harder because it was made clear to me that being sentimental would not be appropriate. I was proud of my self-control and was told that my stoicism was a sign of good manners. I was glad to believe that, as it allowed me to avoid the emotional response to losing my mother.

But the lack of mourning was confusing for me, and the absence of any emotional expression regarding the loss of my mother seemed odd.

1

I could see no way to express my grief, so it was buried within me and I grieved alone. My father went to Italy, staying at a pensione in Assisi. Every day he visited the Giotto murals at the Church of Santa Croce, consoling himself by looking at those great works of art.

While he was away I stayed with my Aunt Lucretia and Uncle Benjamin to give my father time to regain his balance. I was grateful to be away from him. My aunt and uncle had no children, so their house was highly organized, with lunch always at one p.m. precisely. My aunt's and uncle's highly ordered life was hard to get used to, but it was a relief from the morbid silence at my house. Living there gave me stability and predictability, for which I was grateful. Nothing unexpected ever happened and every day after school I stayed out with my friends for as long as I could.

One day while eating lunch, I lifted a spoonful of soup from the edge of the plate nearest to me. My aunt looked at me for a few seconds and said gently, "My dear boy; you haven't forgotten how to eat your soup, have you? As your ship goes out to sea, so your soup goes way from me," she intoned, reminding me of a childhood rule that soup should be lifted from the far edge of the bowl so as not to drip onto one's shirt. She smiled quietly as I ate the remainder of my soup correctly.

I never talked to my father about our loss, which confused me. But as my Aunt Lucretia often said to me, as if to console me in my loneliness, "One must learn to develop an affection for the stiff upper lip, the emotion unvoiced, the desire undeclared, small acts of ceremony, not making too much of things. One must learn, without knowing quite how, that to move in public means a series of encounters and avoidances: how to give money to beggars, how to greet acquaintances without stopping, how to navigate conversations in public without being overheard by strangers."

After several weeks away, my father returned to Dublin unannounced, re-opened our house, found a new housekeeper, and resumed the management of his company, Irish Cement Ltd, a manufacturing plant that had been established by his grandfather in County Limerick. He spent time alone at the family house in County Mayo, acting as though nothing untoward had happened in his life.

Everyone in my father's life assumed the exact position he or she had held before my mother's death. There was Sunday lunch at my father's house with relatives. Fresh flowers re-appeared, cook made our favorite dishes, and my father played cards at home with his cronies and sometimes went to parties. At lunch, my father would ask if I thought the roast was well cooked, and was pleased when I said it was "just right."

I dressed like a junior version of him, wearing well-cut jackets, neatly pressed shirts, and beautiful shoes. At Christmas, my aunt bought presents for everyone, from everyone, so when the gifts were opened one could exclaim with surprise at not only what one had been given, but at what one gave as well. I took all this domestic formality as a matter of course but developed a life that was separate and apart from all that, which revolved around a group of four close friends from school whom I had known since childhood.

When we left our houses for tennis on weekends, we filled our tennis ball cans with foul blends of whiskey and liquor, which we took from every bottle in our fathers' liquor cabinets that was never noticed. Instead of tennis, we went into the woods or to the seashore, drinking, smoking, and regaling each other with stories, jokes, and lewd descriptions of the young ladies we knew. We hated team sports, dismissing them as infantile. So we hid out together and learned to conceal what we regarded as our highly developed intellectuality, lest we be mocked by the sports-mad boys at Belvedere College, our Jesuit high school.

My friend, Presley, was reading Freud, and had an explanation for everything, showing off by using technical terms unknown to the rest of us. He tried to convince my friends and me that understanding our emotional lives was essential, but Presley talked a lot of jargon, and we never figured out what he meant, apart from sensing that the psychological aspects of our lives were a jar of snakes best not to open. We were busy understanding the rules and how to follow them, and too content being good boys to bother about our emotional lives.

My friend, John, was taken with the history of science and knew a lot about Isaac Newton. My friend, Patrick, was the theologian in the group, full of florid denunciations of the Catholic Church and admiration for the intellectualism and financial prowess of the Jews ---not that any of us knew any Jews and neither did our families, but that was enough to recommend them. I was interested in exotic places, mysterious destinations like Saudi Arabia and Palestine.

All through high school, we played bridge every Friday evening until dawn at Presley's house. His father had a collection of classical music on gramophone records. Ever alert to broadening our general knowledge, we listened to a different composer every week as we played cards. After hearing all the records, we started over and played them again.

The music often moved me to tears and became a way to come into contact with my feelings, a kind of "back-channel" to my emotional life. That was not the reaction of my card-playing friends, however, so I was careful not to show the intensity of my response to the music.

I had no idea what to do with my sadness, except to know that it was bad form to "wear one's emotions on one's sleeve," something vulgar and ostentatious that was to be avoided at all costs. Of course that meant I didn't learn anything about emotional life. But those Friday evenings created friendships that lasted all our lives.

My friends and I believed that the measure of ourselves was our cerebral lives. There was nothing about our education or our lives at home that suggested otherwise. As a result, I became used to what Presley called "repressing my feelings." But I was also learning to lie to myself about myself.

I remember being at a party at the house of my friend, John. My friends and I were smoking outside and carefully disposed of the evidence of our naughtiness. When we went indoors, John's grandmother told us how proud she was of us for not having taken up the unattractive habit of using cigarettes. Secrets kept, we thought proudly, we who were only open to each other!

I was developing an image of myself that I was dimly aware was not really me. This secretiveness helped me develop a dual personality - one public and one private. Still, I was dimly aware that emotional life could be interesting, as it certainly had become to my Freud-besotted friend, Presley. But I hadn't the courage to ask him about that. Best to leave well enough alone and muddle through.

Belvedere College was a place where the newly rich or the nearly rich sent their sons, confident that our futures meant joining family businesses and that the Jesuits would keep us from dangerous new political and social ideas. That did not always work.

The renowned Abbey Theatre produced plays with controversial characters and we went to see them. There was Nora in Henrik Ibsen's

"A Doll's House," who rebels against being treated like a woman-child who is made to be dependent on her husband for everything. In the last scene, she leaves her house forever, famously slamming the door in her husband's face and saying proudly, "I have no idea what is to become of me." My three friends and I went to see it and were amazed at the prospect of anyone, especially a married woman, bravely facing an uncertain future alone.

Although we were not at boarding school, the effect was the same. "They are in good hands," our parents often proclaimed, enabling them to avoid monitoring what their boys did and how they spent their time. They also assumed that the priests would tell us what we needed to know about the facts of life, releasing our fathers from that awkward duty. In fact, sex was never mentioned by the priests, except to remind us that masturbation was "self-abuse," using up the same energy as running a mile at full tilt and that a cold shower was the right way to tame our erotic impulses. We knew better, and started masturbating alone and together.

Weekly confession was required at school, and we realized that since all of us went to different confessors, we could share our lists of sins and thereby avoid figuring out what we had done that needed forgiveness. We kept the ruse going for months at a time, with no harm that we could see to our spiritual lives.

The intellectually slow boys at Belvedere studied French or Spanish, branding them as incapable of Latin, Greek or German, languages that we were led to believe were the basis of English and therefore would be useful later in life. I took Latin, German, and French at school and studied Spanish and Arabic with a tutor at home.

When plays were produced at Belvedere College, the school told itself smugly that they were so good that they attracted an audience beyond the school's supporters. In reality, the productions were vaguely interesting schoolboy attempts at Shaw, Sheridan, and Shakespeare. Some plays were forbidden and never considered for production: John Singleton Synge (too political), Strindberg and Ibsen (too radical), Chekov (nothing happens), and Moliere (too risqué). Boys played women's parts and dressed accordingly, which the rest of us took in good spirit.

I performed small parts in plays because my German teacher told the head of the Theatre Department that my voice was deep and theatrical. But shyness and fear of forgetting lines kept me in minor parts. Still, I liked being associated with the atmosphere of the theater, dimly aware that being around theater people might be an antidote to the formality of my life.

So instead of trying to become an actor, I decided to read all the major plays of Western Theater, starting with Aeschylus. I told myself that reading this material would be useful later in life when I would not have time to read extensively. That did not make any sense, of course, but then rationalizations serve purposes other than explaining things, or so Presley, our Freudian expert, told me.

The theatre seemed a respectable way to come into contact with flamboyant personalities. Were there actually people like Hedda Gabler, my favorite theatrical character, bored and repressed, looking for ways to do mischief with accomplices like the evil Judge Brack? There was no one like her in my circle of family and friends, but still, I imagined there must be places in the real world where people actually expressed their emotions, got openly angry or silly, and lived to tell about it.

I was not particularly creative or demonstrative, but the development of my secret self was a comfortable way to conceal my interest in radical or eccentric ideas. I secretly read the Communist Manifesto, Proust, and Stendhal, newspapers like The Daily Worker from London or The New Republic from America, and was avidly interested in radical, social, and political subjects. I read politically unsavory British writers like Elizabeth Gaskill, and loved Abbe de Saint-Real's idea that history "holds up an image of our vices." Despite my mildly eccentric interests, I was a good student and got mostly Academic Firsts in my courses.

I wanted to go to Cambridge University, where my uncle Benjamin had been forty years before. He told me that an Irish background and a Jesuit education would present obstacles to admission, but a letter from him and recommendations from the rector of my school got me admitted to Pembroke College at Cambridge.

My uncle told me about the social conventions at Cambridge, how important it was to know about them, and how certain he was that they had not changed since his day. He said, "Edwin, my boy, there is one thing I must beg of you. Always wear a tall hat on Sundays. It is by that more than anything that a man is judged," advice about which I had doubts. Then he gave me one of his high hats, "not the one I wore at Cambridge but sufficiently old and out of style to let people know you were a gentleman before you got to Pembroke. Never wear a tweed coat and flannels, always a suit. Go to a Dublin tailor, you'll get longer credit. The damp from the River Cam makes for cold winters. You will need sturdy brogues, one in black and one in brown. Go to my boot maker, and he will make them up for you. I hope that this advice has been delivered at a judicious moment. I wish I had more for you, but I haven't."

I took the hat, and his bookmaker's address, thanked him, and left with rising excitement about what to expect. Hats and shoes as the measure of a man struck me as odd but made me intrigued about Cambridge.

I also got information from my uncle's great-nephew who was entering his fourth year at Cambridge. He had been President of the Junior Common Room, an altogether substantial person at Cambridge. Although I barely knew him, I called on him a week before I was to leave for England and stayed for tea. We ate anchovy toast and walnut cake, after which he lit his pipe and laid down rules that I should follow.

"You must read history. The very worst is English Literature and the next worst is Modern Greats. Go only to the best lectures, whether they are in your college or not. People will be wary of you because you are an Irish-Catholic, who all of Cambridge thinks are sodomites with unpleasant accents. Do not get rooms in the front of your college," he told me gravely. "People will start dropping in, drinking your sherry and soon people will think of your rooms as a free bar." I wasn't particularly impressed with his advice, but thanked him.

My father, on the other hand, offered me no advice at all, avoiding, as always, serious subjects. But when I was accepted at Cambridge, he told me, "I have been talking about you. When I was in London last week, I ran into the Earl of Balfour at my club, who has just retired as Chancellor at Cambridge. I asked him what your allowance should be. He said three hundred a year. That's all most men have. I thought that deplorable. At no other time in your life will a few extra pounds make such a difference in your importance and popularity. I toyed with the idea of giving you five hundred," he said, slightly amused, "but should Lord Balfour come to hear of it, it might sound deliberately impolite.

So I shall give you four hundred." I was pleased by his generosity and thanked him for it.

I did get rooms on the first floor, but facing the quad. They were small but with deeply recessed windows and a painted ceiling, and I was glad as a first-year student to get them. I was living in one of the oldest and most picturesque colleges in Cambridge, its common room paneled in oak, lit by candles in silver candlesticks, and heated by a noble fire. But still, I could not avoid the feeling that this sort of luxury was inappropriate at the start of life. We were taught at home and school that good fortune must be earned, but nothing I had done so far had seemed enough. So I determined to be a diligent and sensible student and became a man of solid reading and dry humor. I rowed with the Pembroke Eight and became an excellent cross-country athlete with my college team. I got mostly Firsts and graduated with respectable second class Honors. I was twenty-two, bursting to leave Britain and go to exotic places where I could spread my wings.

A Spanish professor told me about a position as a tutor to the children of Luis Eduardo, 3rd Conde de Villanueva de Granada, one of his former students. A Spanish aristocrat, he lived with his English wife and three children on an estate called Los Olivares in the south of Spain, just north of Granada. He knew of my interest in Arab culture and told me that he would give me a letter of introduction to the Director of the Arabic Studies School in Granada in the hope that I could spend time to do research there. My professor said that scholars who had used its material were impressed with its holdings and the generosity of the curators. It was housed in splendor at the Palace of Charles V, a Renaissance building next to the Alhambra.

There was a school at Los Olivares for the village children. Luis Eduardo wrote that the teacher was a young graduate of the University of Madrid, whom I would assist. In the afternoons, I would be in charge of the education of the family's two boys, Leander and Oscar, nine and seven years old, teaching them English, Latin, French, European history, and math. Their sister, Ottilie, was four years old and would still be under the guidance of her Irish nanny. I would also be in charge of outings on the children's ponies, country walks and swimming in a pond on the estate.

I felt both sophisticated and innocent at the prospect of living in the south of Spain. Its combination of Spanish and Arabic heritage was intriguing, and I happily accepted the appointment.

CHAPTER TWO

My Spanish Adventure Begins

L uis Eduardo sent me a first class ticket from London to Madrid, which I took to be a good beginning for a relationship with an employer whom I had not met. I left London in June, 1931.

The boat train from London was slowed by relentless rain, the crossing from Dover to Ostend harsh. Then to Paris in the early morning with its cheerful, bustling aspect, a promise of delicious coffee and croissants, a positive smell quite peculiar to itself. I took a taxi to the Hotel Terminus Lyon, across from the station. I had a bath, shaved, and lunched early at Fauchon, which was hot and half empty. Rising late the next day, I sat at a little cafe with my bread and coffee while reading my Baedekers Guide to Spain and Portugal. Then I walked for some time through the Marais, looking at its grand 18th century houses in the Place des Vosges. At my uncle's insistence, I ate a dinner of seafood at Prunier. As it had started to rain, I returned to my hotel, lit a fire, and spent the evening in bed drinking whiskey and reading Schiller. The next day was warm and dusty. I went to the Gare de Lyon to catch the train south, which was smooth and fast, the pinewoods passing the windows and a distant view of mountain peaks. There were new uniforms at the Spanish frontier at Irun, morning coffee and bread at the station buffet, and country people around me with Southern grace. From there I went on to San Sebastian, staying for the night at the luxe Hotel Maria Cristina, also paid for by my new employer.

The next day I left for Madrid, outside conifers changing to wheat fields, stands of trees, blue cabbages, and slow moving oxen carts laden with produce. As the sun mounted high, the country glowed with heat. At last, late in the afternoon, arrival in Madrid.

I knew very little about Spain. None of my Cambridge friends had been there. They went to Italy for the sun and Roman antiquities. I was vaguely aware that English investors had built railroads and factories, and had imported sherry since the 16th century made in Spain in distilleries owned by English families. I also knew that there were millions of olive and orange trees, grapes that produced bad wine, and gypsies who sang loud, emotionally overwrought music.

My Baedeker's contained ominous descriptions of traveler's obstacles, dire warnings about thieves and pickpockets, food that was hard to digest because it was cooked in olive oil, and warnings about the hot, dry Spanish climate in the south. Only the best hotels were included, so as to avoid bad ventilation, insect infestation, and lack of cleanliness. I was particularly interested in descriptions of highly emotional reactions to ordinary social situations and the rigid social conventions amongst the upper class. There was also lot in Baedekers about the inherent dignity of Spanish people, the handshakes and embraces, and the gentlemanly courtesies common to all Spaniards. Apparently, social and linguistic false steps by foreigners were treated with grace and generosity.

Luis Eduardo had arranged for me to stay overnight in Madrid with his father, Don Carlo. I arrived at *Charmatin* Station at midday, was met by a chauffeur, and taken to an apartment on the second floor of a building overlooking the Botanical Garden.

Don Carlo was waiting for me at his apartment, smiling broadly as he opened the door and welcomed me. He was tall, a little portly, with longish, disheveled dark hair, full and majestic. His suntanned and wrinkled face suggested a life spent outdoors. He wore the well-cut, well-worn linen jacket donned by the sort of man who dresses for comfort, whether his clothes are in fashion or not. His dark eyes were inquisitive, giving the impression that he was content in old age.

We shook hands. He called for a servant to take my luggage to my room, and we went into a large sitting room, which was hung with gilt-framed paintings and had a quantity of furniture in all sorts of styles and fabrics. The walls were covered in different marbles, "as in Valencia." He showed me photographs of his three grandchildren that he said had been taken by Katherine, his daughter-in-law. French doors opened onto a long balcony overlooking an immense public garden that Don Carlo said proudly was one of the oldest botanical gardens in the world. He told me about his trips to England and his visits to its country house gardens to gather information for the plants he put into what he referred to as his "English Gardens" at Los Olivares.

We sat on the balcony. Tea and sandwiches were brought and we chatted amiably about Dublin where he said he had never been, and my impression of the hotel Maria Christina at San Sebastian, a building he admired for its modernity with telephones and private bathrooms for every room. I told him how comfortable it was, and how grateful I was that his son had arranged for me to stay there, a compliment that pleased him.

He said that lunch would be in about an hour and recommended that I rest before that. I took his advice. He rang for his housekeeper to take me to my room.

I was surprised to have been received with such fullness. I was, after all, only a tutor to Don Carlo's grandchildren. Had such a situation come up at my father's house in Dublin, any guest not part of the family would have been shunted to his room by the housekeeper and told when dinner would be served, without any pretense of welcome or charm.

At lunch I met Begonia, Don Carlo's wife, a beautiful woman some years younger than he, who I came to understand was his second wife. Both spoke excellent English, having been raised, as they told me, by English or Irish nannies, as were children of educated families at that time, even though their parents spoke little English and the nannies spoke almost no Spanish.

Begonia was dressed in a way that my mother would have said was a degree of French perfection, "but sufficiently beautiful to be just visible through her wonderful clothes."

She showed great deference to her new husband. She seemed ostentatious about proper form, correcting the man serving lunch who placed her husband's napkin untidily under his chin, calling for the man about to serve lunch to pull her chair back from the table, rising from her chair to adjust the offending napkin herself. She waited stiffly for the servant to push in her chair so she could be seated, neither looking at him nor thanking him.

Lunch started with three kinds of Spanish ham, thinly sliced, with a few dry oval-shaped hard biscuits and olives. Then came asparagus soup rich with cream. A fish course with potatoes was next, remarkable for the simplicity of its presentation: no sauces, no vegetables, very little seasoning. Then came the cheeses accompanied by a delicious crème-caramel. We drank white wine during lunch and coffee afterwards.

Begonia insisted my plate be kept full, about which I gently protested, inadvertently insulting her by intimating that I did not like Spanish food. She was wrong about my not liking the food, which was simple, elegant, and delicious. But after traveling for three days, I wondered if scrambled eggs, toast, and tea would have suited me better.

Lunch took two hours and was followed by a siesta. I was awakened by a soft knock on my door, after which Don Carlo and I walked in the Botanical Garden, where he pointed out a collection of olive trees of all species from all parts of Spain. He commented delicately on Begonia's overbearing style, which he said came from wanting to be helpful. I could see that, I suppose, but I did not respond because his comments about his wife made me uncomfortable.

I was not used to this sort of intimate family gossip, which would have been unthinkable in Dublin. I would be leaving the next day for Los Olivares and presumed that when I got there, my status in the household would be cleared up. Don Carlos's wife had to be a formidable character in this family if her behavior was being commented on to an outsider barely above the status of a servant.

To my relief, dinner was a simple affair; roast chicken, and some salad followed by fruit, coffee, and reddish colored brandy called *pacharan* which Don Carlo said was from Navarra in the north. I was starting to think that Baedeker's was wrong about Spanish food, which seemed refined and interesting.

I thanked Don Carlo for his kindness at having spent the afternoon with me and said that I was booked on an early train for Granada. Begonia told me that she was surprised and irritated that these arrangements were made without consulting her. She had plans for me to be driven with her to Los Olivares. She told me to give her my ticket and she would get it refunded. She would telegraph Luis Eduardo about this change. It was, of course, impossible to refuse Begonia's offer, although I felt awkward about her changing Luis Eduardo's arrangements and wondered what he would think of this interference.

I was tired but wanted to see a little of Madrid before retiring, so I asked Begonia and Don Carlos if they would mind my taking a walk around the city. I said there was a good map in my Baedeker so I would not get lost. It was nearly dark by this time, and Begonia said that there were sometimes unexpected political manifestations in the streets and that for her peace of mind she would send the butler along with me, to which Don Carlo said with some directness, "Mr. Fitzgerald is a grown man, Begonia, and does not need a chaperone." At that, Begonia stiffened her back, saying archly, "As you wish, Don Carlo, but I will tell a servant to stay up to let in our guest."

Begonia's solicitous treatment of me seemed excessive. Was it an elaborate form of condescension, I wondered? Or was it just that I was in a household that was very different from what I was used to, with people saying things about each other to a total stranger like me? Not Hedda Gabler's house exactly, but I began to imagine the trouble that could be caused when people said exactly what was on their minds!

I was dimly aware of the political changes that had recently taken place. British newspapers had reported ominously that the recent election of a Republican government and the King's departure, but not abdication, had emboldened leftist elements in the society to express their political enthusiasm in public, and I wanted to see some of that if I could. A walk in Madrid at night seemed a good way to do that.

I was disappointed at not seeing raucous demonstrations, but was charmed by the look of Madrid. People strolled arm in arm along the middle of a grand boulevard, and cafes were full of people chatting amiably. My map led me to the Plaza Major, an enormous public space surrounded by beautiful old buildings with arcades below where people window shopped or sat at cafes. I happened across a glamorous Parisian sort of cafe, crowded with people and children, selling cups of dense hot chocolate and *churros*, sticks of fried dough covered with sugar, which I consumed while sitting at a little table along the narrow passage leading to the cafe. After a couple of hours, I returned to Don Carlos's flat. I thanked the maid for waiting up for me; to which she bowed but said nothing. I retired to my room and slept heavily.

The next morning the household was up early, bustling about with luggage, preparing picnic lunches, Begonia barking orders like a general. The mild chaos amused me. When the car was packed up, and we were about to leave, Don Carlo and Begonia took a little walk together, arm in arm, chatting and giggling like young lovers. We would be traveling in a beautiful old Daimler car, ivory in color, bright with nickel, swollen here and there with hatboxes, lunch boxes, and toolboxes. I sat down in a sort of green leather conservatory, and we started.

Begonia filled the day with chatter speaking half in Spanish and half in English, which I barely heard over the noise of the car. The road was good for an hour after leaving Madrid but then became narrow and full of potholes. It was dusty, so the windows were nearly closed. The soil looked unproductive and seemed mostly uncultivated. Hills rolled gently behind each other in shades of brown, tan, and grey. Here and there were little thickets of tall trees planted in rows, thin trunks and pale green foliage that moved gently in the breeze. But mostly the landscape was barren except for herds of sheep.

Distant church towers signaled the existence of villages reached by small roads - tracks really. Now and then we saw peasants slowly walking along the side of the road with their cattle and carts. They greeted the huge car with respect, solemnly removing their hats, and bowing as we drove past, throwing up dust and road gravel. After about four hours, Begonia told the driver to stop near a river, shaded by trees over tall grass. The chauffeur opened the doors, we got out, and he set a table and two chairs with a tablecloth and napkins. Another elaborate lunch, I thought, not shortchanged because we were traveling. There was chilled wine with crystal glasses, and little china plates with silver knives and forks. After lunch, Begonia asked me to come with her to a spot along the river, at the top of an elevated bank with a view toward a village nearby. As we sat, children approached, cautiously staring at us.

"Come here," Begonia said. She gave them grapes, slices of melon, and then some ham, bread, and chocolate. Withdrawing a little way off, they devoured the delicacies with their hands. "These children are too poor to have much to eat. I stop here on every trip south and they know to come to me and get food."

I was touched by the change in Begonia's tone as she talked about these peasant children. Her haughtiness had disappeared. She said, "I was brought up in Murcia, near the Mediterranean coast. The villagers are impoverished there, and I learned from my father to be kind to these creatures. I often go this way, and they have learned to watch for my car and come for delicacies they would never otherwise have."

After the children left, I was surprised when Begonia lay down on a blanket for her half-hour siesta, a straw hat shading her eyes, entirely oblivious of how eccentric that seemed to me.

At mid-afternoon, we stopped at the lovely town of *Ubeda* to stay overnight with Begonia's cousin the *Contessa de Pallavincino*. She greeted Begonia with extravagant kisses, and welcomed us to her house, speaking good English. She was very thin, wore a severe, elegant black dress, and seemed glad to have visitors. She led us through a courtyard surrounded by second-story galleries, into a drawing room with banks of French doors opening onto a terrace, and then into a garden surrounded by deep flower borders with immense trees providing shade.

She invited us to sit on chairs on a perfectly kept patch of lawn, where we were served tea and ubiquitous slices of *jamon* plus olives, bread sticks, little sandwiches on white bread with a creamy filling with the crusts removed, and almond cakes. "Cook made these sandwiches for our young English guest," she said. "I spent summers in Dorset in my youth and loved them, and I have taught cook how to make them, although she will not eat them herself." This little speech pleased Begonia, as though somehow showing me how worldly her friends were.

After a while, I asked to be allowed to take a walk. Baedeker's said the town contained impressive Renaissance houses built with money got by ordinary soldiers who had been posted to the New World. Our hostess was glad of my interest and said I should look at the Cathedral and the Bishop's house next to it, both beautiful buildings in the central plaza with long views of the olive orchards surrounding the town. The day was slowly fading into darkness as I stopped for a glass of wine at a cafe on the plaza, full of stately old gentlemen chatting with their friends while playing cards at tables lit by small oil lamps.

The town was dark as I found my way back to the house. Before I could pull the doorbell, a servant opened the door and took me to a bedroom on the second floor. It had little balconies opening to the street and a bathroom that had been inserted into what had probably been a dressing room. The upholstery on the furniture was a bit shabby, but the atmosphere was charming with numerous electric lamps with faded silk shades and a comfortable bed with a rose-colored silk quilt and linen sheets with the family crest. The man who showed me to the room gave a whiskey and drew a bath in which I soaked for half an hour. The town was quiet, and I slept soundly.

Breakfast was in the courtyard. We were served two beautifully poached eggs on toast, poached the proper way, not little round hard bullets shaped in tin cups. The rolls smelled of fresh bread, the most delicious smell in the world. There was a good-sized round of butter stamped with the family crest, marmalade, honey, and strawberry jam. The coffee was served with a lot of milk and sugar, which even so was too strong for me.

Then we drove through the rolling landscape south of Ubeda with fields of olive trees as far as the eye could see. Another elaborate picnic was laid out in the afternoon. We arrived at Los Olivares in the early evening.

By this time, I had no idea what I had gotten myself into. Begonia had been entirely self-absorbed on the drive south, dropping hints that she was not happy at the state of things at Los Olivares, as though soliciting my friendship. I could not imagine why she would be interested in my opinion, but obviously, she had her reasons. Begonia told me that Los Olivares had a much-admired English garden built by her husband's father. Katherine, her step-daughter-in-law, believed that one could not keep a garden unless one was willing to work in it every day, which she did.

In Dublin, I was sometimes pressed into service in the spring to help my father bring plants from the greenhouse. His specialty was Pelariums, a kind of geranium, and a collection of ancient Peony bushes. He sometimes told me enviously about the greenhouses of the great English gardener, Gertrude Jekyll, at Upton Grey, from which 1,000 hothouse plants would be brought outside in the spring. We took 150 from ours.

I was interested in what an English Garden in Andalusia could be like with its hot climate and what looked like dry soil. Begonia told me that water came through water channels that had been restored by her husband and built during the Arab occupation of Southern Spain. Ancient oak trees shaded the garden.

Begonia reported that Luis Eduardo and Katharine encouraged visitors on weekends, something they had enjoyed doing on Thursday – Tuesday weekends at the country houses of Cambridge friends. Interesting Spanish personalities from politics and the arts were often weekend guests, even some that they did not know well. Staying on for several days was essential because Los Olivares was a long train ride from Madrid.

Begonia told me that she hated these weekends and that all her friends agreed that they were ostentatious and interfered with family life. The guests were generally unknown to her, and she did not like meeting new people. In addition, Luis Eduardo asked his guests to use given names, so she was called Begonia by people she hardly knew, to which silence was the only possible response as it was to the ejaculation of "Cheers" before drinking, or "It was so nice to meet you" after saying goodbye, and the horror of being introduced without any prefix. She tried her best to keep her grandchildren from interacting with the guests, but Luis Eduardo and Katherine often invited the children to meet them before dinner.

As we arrived at Los Olivares, Begonia instructed the chauffeur to lean on his horn. Near the bottom of the drive was a small building which Begonia dismissively described as "my husband's late-first-wife's schoolhouse building," as she ostentatiously crossed herself. We moved slowly up the long driveway through an alley of Oleander and beds of Agapanthus, which gave a bluish light to the shade of the trees. The dogs came to investigate, bristling and noisy with self-importance.

Closer to the entrance of the house was a gypsy caravan painted in bright colors with its doors swung open, apparently a place for the children to play. There were several cars parked at the side of the driveway. One was a huge black sedan with the doors open and a driver in uniform standing beside it smoking a cigarette, along with smaller cars, including a yellow convertible with the top down. I was intrigued that one of the weekend parties might be underway.

Begonia became silent as we approached the house. When we were almost there, she blurted out, "They might have told me that there would be one of their infernal weekend house parties. Do you see that huge black car? It belongs to Cardinal Segura, an uncle of my husband. He and Luis Eduardo have taken a liking to each other and he often comes for weekends. God knows who else is here. What vulgar creature would drive that immense yellow car? I suspect it's that Constantia de

La Mora. Her grandfather was a Spanish Prime Minister, but she revels in social and political eccentricities. On top of that she dresses badly."

Suddenly Begonia gripped my arm and looked directly at me. "Young man, you will do well to stay as far away from these visitors as you can. Spain is now in the midst of political changes and social troubles, and the less you come into contact with these new political ideas, the better."

It took all my self-control not to tell Begonia that I intended to do just the opposite, but being a self-effacing British gentleman, I stayed silent. I had come all this way looking for opportunities to immerse myself in a new culture, and it seemed ever more likely that I would meet interesting people, even at a remote place like Los Olivares.

Just then the driver swung round in front of the door, as Luis Eduardo and Katharine were coming out to meet us. Three children jumped down from the caravan and ran to our car, opening the doors when they got there. Begonia was helped from the back of the car, gave kisses to the children who were happy to see her, expecting and getting presents that Begonia had carried on the seat beside her from Madrid. Katherine raised her eyebrows at that but kept quiet. Proper English reticence I thought. How nice!

Begonia interrupted the greetings from the children with a remark to the oldest child that there were stains on his shirt, provoking a look of exasperation from Katherine, after which the children promptly disappeared into the gypsy caravan to look at their presents.

Luis Eduardo and Katherine introduced themselves to me and then had our luggage unloaded. Begonia and Katherine disappeared into the house, leaving me standing next to Luis Eduardo on the gravel drive-way. He was tall with fine dark eyes, very tanned, his hair perfectly cut.

He was wearing a white shirt open at the neck, a short cotton jacket, jodhpurs and riding boots. He smiled warmly as he shook my hand. I was glad of his informality and liked him immediately.

He welcomed me to Los Olivares and said, "You look well enough after spending two days on the road in Begonia's company. I hope it wasn't too tiresome, and that Begonia did not regale you with gratuitous comments about your appearance, something she does all the time, as though if unable to express herself the moment a thought occurs, she will forget it and thereby lose an opportunity to be what she thinks of as being helpful. It's one of her worst habits."

"Oh, no, sir, there was none of that," I said, fully aware that I did not want to be drawn into a conversation about Begonia.

"Please call me Luis Eduardo and my wife Katherine. We are very informal here, even though Begonia would like it to be otherwise. If you are up to it let's take a walk so you can get yourself oriented to the place. My man will take you to your rooms where you should rest a little before we go. While your things are being unpacked we can take our walk."

At that, a young servant appeared and led me to the second floor. He opened the door to a little sitting room that contained a round table with an embroidered cloth, a bookcase, a chest of drawers, several lamps, an old Turkish rug on the floor, and a comfortable chair near a balcony that overlooked the olive groves. There was an adjoining bedroom from which I could see the top of a village church.

He asked me if I wanted a bath and I said yes, so he took me into a room with a marble floor, a huge soaking tub with a silver shower head above it, a marble sink, and a large table covered in sheets facing a pair of French doors looking over the olive orchards. He drew a bath as I studied the view. When he left, I got in the tub and soaked for a while, showered, dried myself, and returned to my rooms. After a rest, I went downstairs. Luis Eduardo was waiting for me in the sitting room. We shook hands and left through the front door, strolling down the drive with two energetic dogs joining us, barking, sniffing, and running enthusiastically back and forth.

"I hope your room is comfortable, Edwin."

"It is, sir. It's charming and has lovely views over the village.

"I have 140,000 olive trees here in 700 acres, some of them hundreds of years old, along with a stand of Alcornocalian oak trees.

I should tell you that a few friends are here for the weekend. Katharine and I go to Madrid every few months to maintain contact with friends and invite them to visit us. When I was at Cambridge, I often spent weekends at friends' parents' country houses and came to admire that tradition. It is quite a foreign thing in Spain to entertain anyone but family or old friends that way, but these house parties are the centerpiece of life for us. I am not sure that we would live here without a stream of visitors. We invite people who have opinions on matters of the day and make them comfortable with long walks in the countryside, good food and drink, lawn tennis on our makeshift court, and bridge in the evenings. If we had bird shooting, it would be like a Friday to Monday in the wilds of Norfolk. By the way, just to show you how English we have become, I should tell you that we observe the English country house custom of not shaking hands at breakfast."

We circled back to the house, walking past the stables, the kitchen garden, and a little building that he told me he had built as a studio for his wife. We entered the house through the loggia at the back.

As we entered the house Luis Eduardo asked me, "Do you play bridge, Mr. Fitzgerald? We often need a fourth because many Spaniards do not play."

I took his calling me by my last name to indicate the differences in our status. "Yes, I do. I learned at Dublin, then at Cambridge got in with a bridge crowd who played incessantly. It consumed too much time so I opted out, but in the process learned something about bidding and sending signals that I had a bad hand, or good hand when I had the reverse."

"Good. Then I hope you won't mind being pressed into a game now and then."

"No sir - I mean, Luis Eduardo, sir. I will try my best, but I may not be as good as you and your guests".

"That won't be a problem. My guests play at all sorts of levels."

"Then I would be glad to help out," I said.

"Tonight at dinner you will meet our great friend, Constancia de la Mora. She is getting divorced, the first to do so under our new government which has legalized divorce amongst the other things they are changing. She comes often; we are always glad to see her and hear the latest gossip from Madrid, where she knows everyone. To the dismay of her aristocratic family, Constancia is leftist politically, is very outspoken, and has become notorious to people like Begonia.

She brought along Mercedes Sanz-Bachiller, an old friend of hers and Katherine's who has founded an organization called Auxilio Social which supports impoverished mothers and children regardless of their political or religious or cultural affiliations: gypsies, unwed mothers, socialists, fascists - none of that matters to her if there are children in need.

"Our other guest is Pedro Segura y Saenz, Cardinal-Archbishop of Toledo, who is my godfather. He is also Papal Nuncio to Spain and an outspoken opponent of everything that the new government is intending to do. But he has a jolly personality and has become a good friend of mine. This kind of friendship, between people who hold strongly differing political opinions, is rare nowadays. There are 25 political parties in Spain, so everyone can find their political niche and stop talking to people who think differently."

I listened with growing excitement at the prospect of meeting such interesting people. Fancy having dinner with a cardinal and a divorcee at the same table! Perhaps I would run into a Spanish Hedda Gabler before long!

After spending so much time with Begonia, and being puzzled by her ramblings, it was a relief that Luis Eduardo and his wife, Katherine, seemed to be intelligent, charming people, unpretentious, ordinary even.

I went to my rooms to rest a little and dress for dinner, which Luis Eduardo told me would be informal. For me, that meant a tweed jacket, dark trousers, open-necked linen shirt, and my best English shoes.

As I was coming down the stairs, I met Katherine dressed simply in a gray silk shirt, a black skirt with a cunning little slit up the back, and no jewelry. Begonia came down a little later looking as though she intended to spend the evening at a casino, wearing elaborate bracelets, a satin skirt, long and rustling, a white silk blouse with deep décolleté and ropes of pearls. She greeted me profusely and we went into the sitting room together. She picked a glass of chilled vermouth with an orange slice, sat on a sofa, and asked me to join her there. I shot a questioning look at Katherine, who indicated that I was on my own.

Sra. de la Mora walked in wearing a short summer dress, no jewelry and black espadrilles. Her hair was drawn back into a bun at the nape of her neck. She looked immensely glamorous to me. Greeting Katherine with kisses, she picked up a glass of champagne and sat next to Begonia. Her friend, Mercedes, entered wearing a dowdy brown suit, with a white shirt. Her hair was cut short and held back from her face with metal hair-clips. On her shoulder was a large emerald broach of the sort inherited from relatives but now entirely out of style, an oddly chosen ornament for an informal weekend in the country.

At that point Luis Eduardo and the Cardinal Segura came in from the loggia, talking intensely. The cardinal was wearing a black sweater over a white shirt, dark brown corduroy trousers, and well-worn peasant-sandals made from raffia and string. Luis wore an old tweed jacket, a pale-blue cotton shirt, dark-colored corduroy trousers, and well-shined boots. Shortly after that the nanny brought in the children. Leander, eight, and Oscar, seven, both very tall for their ages, were wearing long-sleeved flannel shirts, cotton trousers and leather sandals. Their hair was combed and their hands and faces were clean. Ottilie wore a pale blue shirt and a colorful skirt, her long blond hair braided and held with a white ribbon. She was wearing traditional raffia sandals with ribbons tied around her legs.

They went to Begonia and kissed her. She pointed out to Oscar that his shirt was wrinkled and had a stain on it. He turned away frowning and looked at his mother, who smiled and said, "Don't worry, darling, it will come out in the wash." They then shook hands with the other guests. Katherine introduced me to Nanny Coleman and to the children, with the boys bowing in an old-fashioned way, their hands held against the seams of their trousers as they stood before me, the little girl curtsying awkwardly. They sat next to Begonia and looked shyly at me, the stranger, their new tutor.

A Moroccan-style leather cushion was in front of the sofa, so I went there and sat on it. The children softened the intensity of their staring a little. I said in English that I was glad to meet them and to be at Los Olivares. They did not answer. I took from my pocket gifts for the children - three polished sea stones each streaked in a different color. I gave one to each of them and told them that they were from the seacoast in Ireland, where I was born. They were impressed that each rock had one of the children's names painted on it, which I told them I had done myself.

Ottilie asked how I knew their names. Leander said with older-brother-condescension, "Papa must have told them to Mr. Fitzgerald." They thanked me, shook my hand, their nanny collected them, and they quietly left the room.

Sra. de la Mora had been carefully watching me with the children. "How charming and clever of you to put their names on rocks," she said, rising to collect a fresh glass of champagne.

"Yes," said Katherine. "Both boys have rock collections, mostly interesting bits of gravel, really, which they keep in old Cuban cigar-boxes they get from their grandfather. Now they have something special."

"In Spain, a child's gift must be simple and straightforward," Begonia called out from her seat, "not wrapped up like a box of chocolates, and it can't cost much. It's *the beauty of gesture* that matters in Spain, not the gift itself, Mr. Fitzgerald."

Everyone was a bit taken aback by this pretentious little speech. Beauty of gesture was obviously something important, but in what way was not clear to me. To my surprise, my little stones were seen as something with more meaning than I thought they would have. Being a student, I could not afford anything extravagant; being a man I would never have thought of wrapping it; traveling light I could not have brought anything fragile.

Cardinal Segura and Luis Eduardo had settled themselves on chairs near Begonia, Constancia, and Mercedes. Katherine went outside to the loggia, and I joined her. She turned and looked directly at me. "Ah, Mr. Fitzgerald, our young Irish gentleman. How nice of you to come here to teach my children. You do not look the worse for having spent two days traveling with Begonia. She is a particular kind of Spanish lady, direct to a fault, in love with her own voice, chatting on relentlessly about nothing in particular. Although I admire her in some ways, she is a woman of little information and uncertain temper. When she is out of sorts, she fancies herself 'nervous.' The business of her life is visiting and gossip." She looked at me directly as she spoke, smiling slightly, almost conspiratorially, I thought.

I suppose I felt flattered by Katherine's directness about Begonia, but also a little put off that our first conversation would be about something so personal. At my house in Dublin I was used to talking about more-or-less nothing, so Katherine's comments about her stepmother-in-law were unexpected. I decided to respond in kind."I did notice her strong personality. One can hardly miss that. But she was kind and lively on our trip."

"What do you mean, she was kind? Something more than good manners?"

I told Katherine about giving food to the local peasants during our picnic stop after leaving *Ubeda*, something Begonia told me she managed to do every time she drove to Los Olivares. Katherine listened intently. "How nice of her, and how odd that this is the first I have heard of it. Begonia is...how shall I say it... an interesting and complicated personality."

At that point, a manservant came up to the doorway and said that dinner was about to be served. Begonia was waiting for me when Katherine and I went inside. She inserted her arm into mine, and I took her into dinner. I found myself looking at a table with a profusion of silver and crystal, and place cards, a surprise, since Luis Eduardo had told me that dinner would be informal. That part, at least, I was accustomed to, dinner where everyone was told where to sit. Luis Eduardo was at the head of the table, Katherine the other end. I thought my table manners would be all right, but I was intrigued and a little apprehensive about what sort of conversation would be expected between a cardinal and a divorcee. I had never met people of that sort, let alone sat at dinner with them, and further, being expected to talk in Spanish.

Begonia's voice sailed out across the table. "Traveling with you was a distinct pleasure, dear boy. Mr. Fitzgerald and I chatted about lots of things on the way, didn't we? Cook packed picnics, the roads were not too awful, and the weather was warm, but not unbearable. Didn't you think so, Mr. Fitzgerald? You would never have survived on the train. Spanish trains are not used by people like us, if you don't mind my putting it that way."

"Quite understandable, Ma'am," I said.

"Oh, please don't call me that. It makes me sound like a shopkeeper's wife or Queen Victoria, neither of which flatters me. You may call me anything but that."

Those are the last things you are, I thought. "What I meant to say is that I appreciate your kindness to have spared me the long train ride, and for that I am grateful."

Katherine gave me a sympathetic look. "What would you like Mr. Fitzgerald to call you, Begonia?" she asked.

"Mr. Fitzgerald can call me La Senora if he wishes," she said with a sly smile. She went on. "What one is called is important in Spain, where everyone is intensely aware of everyone else's position in the aristocratic hierarchy. Our dozen or so Grandees are the oldest, richest and care most about their position. But there is none of the formality of the British aristocracy, where dukes speak to barons with condescension, in recognition of their lesser status. Barons accept that, because they, in turn, speak to their inferiors that same way. In Spain, status is indicated in more subtle ways. I, for example, have lived in Madrid with Luis Eduardo's father for only about ten years, but in that short time I have become someone everyone wants to invite. There are more invitations to balls and dinners than we could ever accept. My parents only accepted invitations where the hostess was from an aristocratic family as distinguished as ours. That was not easy, as King Philip V ennobled my family in 1715. But I am not snobbish and go where I please, something my friends admire as a modern way of behaving."

There was something ominous about this little speech, as though Begonia needed to remind everyone that her position in this household required deference. The thought flashed through my mind that if my friend, Presley, were there, he would apply what he thinks of as his great knowledge of Freud to explain this odd pronouncement from Begonia, her second of the evening.

When she stopped, there was a little silence, after which Luis Eduardo turned to me and asked if I had noticed anything unusual about the evening light and then said, "An acquaintance of mine from Granada, called Garcia Lorca, writes that in this part of the world dusk lasts forever. As the sun goes down, the landscape is transfigured, first falling into lavender pools of shadow, then into deep blue and, at last, violet, and for a moment or two the night takes on the color of bruised bodies."

"Oh, for heaven's sake, Luis, why do you want to tell Mr. Fitzgerald about that peculiar friend of yours? He may fancy himself a good writer, as you tell me he is, but he is also a communist, and I cannot abide people who want to get rid of our way of life."

The man serving dinner entered the dining room and flourished napkins onto our laps. Another man poured white wine into tall glasses, then poured water into larger ones. The dishes were old Sevres, a little chipped, with wide gilded borders. The silver was monogrammed with a cipher intertwining the letters L-O for Los Olivares.

I was horrified when the Cardinal, sitting directly across from me, asked me something in Spanish, speaking fast. I got the gist of it, which was about my journey from Madrid and I was able to answer decently in Spanish. He smiled at me and said, "Luis, you've got a quick one here, knowing Spanish well enough. How did you find him?"

"I didn't find him, Pedro; he found me, through his knowing my old professor at Cambridge, Valdez-Moreno. You remember him, don't you? He was here last year, so he knew that I have school-age children, and I told him that I wanted him to find me a tutor."

"Instead of sending them to that school your mother Louisa started in the village?" the Cardinal asked sardonically.

Katherine interrupted. "The boys will be at that school in the mornings and here with Mr. Fitzgerald in the afternoons."

"Ah, I see. So the influence of the church is nowhere to be had. And what about mass, communion, confession and their eternal salvation? Who tells them about that?"

"Monsignor Alberto comes from the village on Wednesday afternoons to instruct them in the faith," said Katherine dryly.

"And, by the way, my dear Katherine, church precepts demand that all education, public and private, must conform to church doctrine."

Luis Eduardo looked directly at his friend, the Cardinal. "That will be taken care of when Leander is twelve years old and goes to the Jesuits at *Colegio San José* in Badajoz, where I was at school, and Oscar will follow him a year later."

"Ah, well, yes," he replied, "The Jesuits, so modern, so intellectual, so avaricious and clever at hiding their millions in real estate and shares in foreign corporations. As the old saying goes, night and Jesuits always return." At that, the Cardinal leaned across the table a little and said, "What do you think, Begonia? Do you think the boys will be set on the right path?"

Just then soup was being served. Begonia waved away the man serving, smiled at Katherine and said, "Katherine and Luis Eduardo, my stepson--"

"Thank you for getting my title right, Luis Eduardo interrupted, "and calling me your *step*son-in-law, Begonia."

Begonia resumed her speech, chastened and irritated, "Yes, well, of course one must be accurate in these things. Still, Luis and Katherine will tell me, again, that it's none of my business, but for the life of me I cannot see the good of sending children away to school, another of those infernal English habits. I have never left Spain, so my ideas are old-fashioned. Even so, what good can come from expecting your children to manage on their own at a boarding school? It should also be obvious that nothing good comes from your children meeting the unconventional people like those you invite to these house parties of yours."

"Oh, for heaven's sake, Begonia, can you never cease to say the same things over and over?" Katherine interrupted sharply, "I am English, and my husband was educated at Cambridge, so we have English ways. Do get past that, won't you? Say what you like, of course, just don't say it over and over again every time you get a chance. Try finding something amusing to say, so if you say it twice we will enjoy it twice."

During this exchange, I glanced at Sra. de la Mora. She seemed to be enjoying herself. Slowly and deliberately, she said, "Katherine, my dear, one can be sure that Begonia is referring to me, someone who actually speaks with your children even though I am about to become a divorced woman. Divorce, now that's one the many things that Spain will have to get used to, don't you think, your Eminence?"

At that, I was frozen with astonishment. What a thing to say to a Cardinal sitting across the dinner table! I had never met a divorced woman and from the look on his face, I doubted that the Cardinal had either. But there she was, chatting sweetly, her demeanor calm and focused, talking about her divorce as if she was talking about a recent film she had seen.

The Cardinal looked at her severely. "My dear Sra. de la Mora, I dare say that your divorce is something that everyone is talking about. Something of a special mark, of which I suppose you are especially proud. I know a little about modern times, having spent some time in Vienna with its obsession about newness in everything: odd music, uncomfortable furniture, buildings without a scrap of decoration, people commissioning portraits of themselves from modern painters who make them look deranged, plus, of course endless gossiping at their cafes. It's mostly newness for its own sake from what I could tell, and to be new is something of a badge of honor amongst the Viennese.

"They have a madman named Freud who talks to people who are nervous or depressed. He says that as they talk the sources of their maladies are revealed and then he writes books about them. So you see, I do know a little about modern times. And please also do not talk idly to me about divorce, Sra. de la Mora. Your uncle has talked to me about how horrified your family is about that. It seems that everyone in your family but you believe that marriage is a sacrament and not subject to civil dissolution."

"I expect it would surprise you to know that I started out as a parish priest at a poor parish in Burgos so I know something about the lower classes, and I take discreet vacations in a little town in the North called *Ezcaray*. Don't assume I have lived all my life in a dreary Episcopal Palace. I come here for weekends because I know that I will meet people with opinions other than my own. We all know that Spain's future is in a state of flux, and because of that I want to understand what people are thinking, and if I can, to find out why they believe what they do. And I am sure that Spain will never want a leftist government for long. In Spain the self-interest of the individual is paramount, and there is no tradition of making a marriage of convenience to have a well-governed society."

There was an awkward silence until Mercedes spoke up: "I must say it always surprises me that socialistic ideas are thought of as such a radical thing in Spain. Surely we all know that in the north, where

I come from, we follow an old communal land system that has always supported community activities that benefit everyone. Our municipality provides for the surgeon, the blacksmith, the apothecary's shop, and it pays for religious indulgences and litanies, as well as salt and seed corn. We also have a cooperative store as well as a municipal credit fund from which villagers can draw loans. All lands are held in common and the income from renting them is divided up in the village fairly and justly. Indeed, the Spanish missions in the New World are often referred to as socialist societies."

The Cardinal followed Mercedes' comments closely and seemed to relish making a response. "My dear Senora, I am delighted to meet some-one who is so well-informed about the socialistic structure in villages in Asturias and other parts of the North. I am also surprised that you would not notice the difference between the operation of organizations that benefit a village and the complexities of trying to govern an entire nation on those principles. One has nothing to do with the other. You are aware, I am sure, that the recent election that brought socialists to power has so many different parties that it will be impossible to form a government that takes into account Spain's wildly diverse opinions and intentions."

Mercedes rose to the occasion. "Your Eminence is probably correct that Spain's Republican experiment may not be able to change the current system, even though it has been corrupt for as long as one can remember."

"You are correct about our current political system," the Cardinal replied, "But accepting a Republican government was more than the king could stomach, so the king went to Italy without actually abdicating. Now the people of Spain think they are in charge."

At this point, the soup dishes were cleared from the table, and the serving people left the room. Luis Eduardo and Katherine were calm and interested in the conversation. I was astonished. Sra. de la Mora smiled at the Cardinal and said, "Well, your Eminence, I am glad to hear about your adventures in the world we all live in, and of your concern about my divorce. Perhaps you also know about an educational program called *Misiones Pedagogicas*. Do you?"

"No, I do not."

Sra. de la Mora then said, "As I suppose you know, my friend Fernando De los Rios was one of the founders *of* the *Institucion Libre de Ensenya*, modern schools that encourage intellectual curiosity, where I studied before going to St. Mary's, Cambridge. De Los Rios is now Minister of Education, and told me that he wants to establish a program called *Misiones Pedagogicas* that will bring cultural artifacts to the most remote villages: full-size copies of paintings in the Prado, recordings of classical composers like Bach and Albeniz, a portable stage for productions of Shakespeare and Lope de Vega, and a library of several hundred books, which remain in the village, along with gasoline-fueled electrical-generators and radios."

"They will also explain the political structure of Spain, comparing us to other European countries, and they will talk about how to decide for whom to vote." Looking at the Cardinal, she continued. "You do realize that none of the children in the Villanueva de Granada are likely to have held a book in their hands, nor seen a film, nor heard the name Valazquez?"

"If I may, Katherine," Sra. de la Mora went on, "let me tell your young man from Dublin that the *Residencia de Estudiante*, is a prestigious cultural institution at the University of Madrid that fosters an intellectual environment for Spain's brightest young thinkers, writers, and artists. Luis Eduardo's friend, Lorca, lived there when he was a student. Katherine told me that the new schoolteacher she has hired lived at the *Residencia*."

Begonia stared at Luis Eduardo and then Katherine, after which she entered the conversation, agitated and loud. "What good can come from raising our peasant's hopes about their futures? Instruction about politics and voting indeed! They will get the idea that people want them to have lives that are different from what their parents have had for centuries! Will it never end, this interference from the coffee-house statesmen in Madrid! Imagine wanting to teach peasants to read and give them a radio to listen to!"

The Cardinal stiffened his back. "Ah, yes, and next women will be voting. Their confessors will tell them who to vote for, under pain of sin if they vote otherwise. Sixty percent of Spaniards cannot read, ladies and gentlemen, so they will vote as they are told and be grateful for that advice."

Just then the next course was brought in and everyone stopped talking. White wine was poured. There was rice with mushrooms, and finally fish roasted in parsley oil. Baedeker mentioned a Spaniard's affection for good food, but this dinner, which in this household seemed to be nothing out of the ordinary, was impressive. Dinner at my father's house in Dublin would have been dried-up roast beef and Yorkshire pudding, tasteless green beans, and apple crumble for the sweet.

Everyone was eating quietly, and I sensed that the conversation needed a jolt. So after the servers left the room, and there was a long, tense silence as we ate, I decided to say something. Looking to the left and right, I said rather too ostentatiously, "Is there salt?"

Luis Eduardo laughed out loud and raised his glass to me. The Cardinal looked at me too, surprised and amused. Begonia stared earnestly at her plate. Katherine patted my arm. Sra. de la Mora smiled conspiratorially at what I thought might be admiration for my inadvertent wit, impressed that I knew how to loosen up stalled dinner conversation.

After dinner, we went to the loggia facing the garden. *Pacharan* was served. By then everyone was chatting about nothing in particular, so I excused myself to go for a walk, feeling that I had acquitted myself decently with my salt question.

I went through the sitting room to the front door, stepped outside, lit a cigarette, and walked down the drive. The evening was illuminated by pale white light from the moon, which, I noted, was nearly full.

When I got back, I went to my room. A servant had turned down my bed and lit a gas lamp, which I turned down as I sat in the darkened room looking through the French doors into the intense blackness of the night, contemplating the events of the day. The moon cast mysterious shadows among the tops of trees. It was intensely quiet.

I came to Spain expecting to find new things. I certainly had never met anyone like Begonia, or a cardinal, or a divorced woman, never mind that I also had to talk in Spanish. It was dawning on me that living at Los Olivares could be an opportunity for me to become less of the shy English gentleman that I had become, and more able to take conversational risks, less insular and smug. I was a very good talker, and listening to my own talk had become the fundamental way I figured things out about myself. But I was also dimly aware that my talking skills had become a barrier to making emotional connections and often left me isolated and served as an excuse to avoid taking initiatives. I cannot count the number of times I talked myself out of having sex by blathering on until the girl in my bed would fall asleep, and then so would I, bewildered by what had not happened.

Talking a lot was also a barrier to making emotional connections with people. I often told myself smugly that people would never know the "real me." At Los Olivares people expressed opinions with no apparent interest in calibrating remarks to suit their audience. I wondered at the impact on people's relationships from being so straightforward. For me, this Spanish directness seemed like a kind of theatre.

The continuous chatter in the house, with people talking over each other or having occasional emotional outbursts, meant to me that they used words for different reasons than I did. The verbal sparring between people, even when there was no disagreement, was constant. Having the last word seemed more prized than actual communication. People sometimes said things like "it's only words" as though the gesture of talking was mainly an exercise in one upmanship. The agitated way that people spoke, and the accompanying gesticulation was often what mattered most, not the meanings of the words. This way of communicating was new to me. I was, of course, hopelessly inept at it.

I wondered if there wasn't a lot of forgiving-and-forgetting in Spain as a way of moving on from disagreements. Perhaps they were just rhetorical flourishes. Holding my own in the face of such directness would take time. But I was determined to try, even if I would occasionally make a fool of myself. Still, I was grateful for everyone's kindness to me. Begonia and her husband treated me very well in Madrid. I was starting to settle in comfortably at Los Olivares, and the people I was meeting were exceptionally interesting.

Baedeker had been full of warnings about eating in Spain: too much oil, too many fried dishes, mediocre wine, undercooked vegetables, and dangerous water. I was unprepared for the refinement of the food and the simplicity of its presentation, both at Begonia's flat and at dinner tonight. Begonia's insistence that I eat more than I wanted was overbearing, but she was also graceful in allowing me to say no without seeming to be offended. She impressed me with her generosity to the poor children who came up to us while we were having lunch on the way, and I was glad to be able to say something complimentary about Begonia during my little chat in the garden with Katherine, and was touched at Begonia's modesty at not having told Katherine herself.

As I thought back on Begonia's remarks and her behavior at dinner, I wondered if she had been trying to convince me of something, to make me her ally in the disagreements with Luis Eduardo and Katherine, or as Begonia called her "my foreign-stepdaughter-in-law." She was a strong presence at Los Olivares, and there was already a bond of affection between us, although I also sensed that it was dangerous to get too close.

From what I could tell from the conversation at dinner, the election of a Republican government was causing a great deal of political and social uncertainty. Being divorced in Spain was apparently shocking. In Dublin, my father and his Catholic friends did not exactly accept divorce, but the religious ostracism that divorced persons faced was their own dilemma. The cardinal had been clearly incensed at the prospect of divorce, and God knows what other coming changes would offend him. But he had the good sense to visit Luis Eduardo's house and meet his friends. I was to learn later how unusual it was in Spain for people of differing opinions to even become acquaintances, never mind friends.

With all these thoughts in my head, I went to bed and 'slept the sleep of the just' as my old Auntie would call it.

CHAPTER THREE

The Next Day

I awoke early the next morning, the conversations at dinner the previous night ringing in my ears, wondering what to expect on my first full day at Los Olivares. I was relieved that my Spanish had held up enough for me to follow the spirited conversation between Cardinal Segura and Sra. de la Mora, and the back and forth between him and Mercedes Sans-Bachillar. I loved it when Begonia entered the conversation whenever it suited her, whether she had anything to add or not. What a boiling pot and how exciting to be here!

I showered in the bathroom on the floor below, shaved and carefully combed my hair, thinking about a friend who had been to Italy and told me about *sprezzatura*, the Italian art of dressing casually. I expected to find something of the same in Spain. I made do with old brown corduroys, sturdy boots, and a fresh cotton shirt with a black silk scarf tied around my neck. In that kit, I went downstairs.

Before going in to breakfast, I decided to have a look at the house. At the bottom of the main staircase was an oval entrance hall with a pair of doors that stood open, a thin embroidered curtain moving gently in the breeze. An archway opened into a spacious drawing room with a bank of French doors surrounded by gold colored, red fringed curtains, opening onto a covered loggia, beyond which was the large well kept lawn and garden.

Floors were highly polished wood partly covered with old Spanish rugs. Small tables stood here and there, many with electric lamps made from silver candlesticks or Chinese pots, all with silk shades of ivory-colored pleated silk, some deteriorating from age. There was a table with carved legs surrounded by three French armchairs covered in ivory and grey striped silk, a "touch of the French," as my aunt would say.

A pair of black, highly polished, bulbous-shaped chests of drawers, perhaps ebony, stood on either side of the chimney piece. Over the chests were hung a matched pair of looking glasses in ornate gilt frames. A sofa was covered in faded cotton slipcovers with a huge glass table in front. Bibelots, ceramic dishes, and stacks of books were on the table and piled underneath it. Nearby there were two elaborate armchairs covered in a blue velvet fabric that looked as though it had been left out in the rain to give it a patina, an old English decorating trick. An archway opened into a dining room, where a crystal chandelier, interspersed with blue crystals, hung over the center of the dining table. The chairs looked to be Chippendale, their seats covered in dingy yellow leather. Black and white family photographs in simple frames hung on the dark olive green walls. The French doors were surrounded by blue and white striped taffeta curtains which opened onto the loggia running along the back of the house. The whole effect was of the sort of modest English country house that is so admired for its deliberately offhand style.

At the far end of the dining room was the breakfast room. I went in to find Katherine at the table with coffee and a toasted roll slathered in crushed tomatoes. She greeted me nicely, and I gave her a deep bow in deference to the house rule of not shaking hands at breakfast, and then went to the breakfast buffet. Instead of the austere coffee-with-bread breakfast that one found on the continent, the sideboard held scrambled eggs, toast in a silver rack, crushed tomatoes to put on the toast, piles of oranges, jams, and marmalade, smoked fish, and oatmeal with brown sugar and cinnamon. There was a huge Spanish ham clamped into a mechanism that held it firmly for slicing off thin pieces using a razor-sharp knife held in a silver holder. A dish contained the type of fried dough I had eaten in Madrid, next to a bowl of sugar to be sprinkled over them.

Katherine saw me eyeing them. "Those *churros* are made fresh here every day. In Madrid, they are bought from a nearby *churreria,* but here cook makes them, using an implement that Begonia brought, a miniature pump that squeezes the dough out by the yard. They are dipped into coffee or chocolate. As you might imagine, the children love them, but so do Luis Eduardo and Begonia because that was their nursery food. They are also a great favorite of our foreign guests. Begonia insists that our guests have them as an alternative to what she calls our 'indigestible English breakfasts.'"

I put two *churros* on my plate, poured a cup of hot chocolate, sat down next to Katherine, and plunged a *churro* into the chocolate which was so thick the little pastry sticks stood up straight.

Sra. de la Mora came into the breakfast room wearing riding boots and jodhpurs, a wide-brimmed fedora and a black shirt, fanning herself with a simple black fan, perspiring slightly after her morning ride. She got coffee and sat next to me. "Ah, Mister Fitzgerald you made quite an impression on the Cardinal last night with your good Spanish, and on me with your witty comment about the salt just at the moment when the conversation needed warming up. Segura is not easily impressed and was probably surprised to find himself taken by the likes of a mere tutor, Cambridge educated or not. He is used to grander connections, like his friendship with King Alfonso, now forever departed from Spain, who managed to leave behind his long-suffering English wife for a few days, and they have now joined Alfonso in Rome where, no doubt, an immense fortune awaits them."

"Segura's fellow churchmen don't like him because he flaunts his royal connections and speaks his mind," Katherine said, "Two weeks after the proclamation of the Second Republic, Segura showed his independence by writing a now notorious pastoral letter that he had published in the Madrid newspapers, denouncing the new government and demanding that the king be brought back from exile. It takes courage to oppose the new government in writing and doing so showed Segura to be a fine exponent of Spanish Catholicism's self-righteousness. As the old saying goes, Spanish Catholics have learned to follow their priests with either a candle or a club."

It was invigorating to have people so far above my station talk to me. It was becoming ever more apparent that the social atmosphere at Los Olivares was so informal that one could actually say anything, to anyone, about anything. Was this custom a kind of informality, or gossip, or something else? I thought about my friend, Presley, and his assertion that

Freud believed everything had more than one meaning, and that these multiple meanings could be known. Was Begonia's aggressive behavior toward Katherine just a lapse of good manners, or was she masking a more complicated agenda, or was I just having trouble understanding a society where everyone so openly spoke their minds? It seemed to me that the Cardinal himself could enter the dining room, take up some toast and jam, sit next to me and start a conversation, plain as that. I supposed that if I asked him to bring me a *churro* he would, and we would soon be calling each other by our given names. I decided to tell Presley to send me books about Freud.

As I was thinking about all this, Luis Eduardo and the Cardinal came in from the garden. I loved that Segura was wearing a comically unsuitable hat with a wide brim in such bad condition that one would never have the nerve to wear it in Dublin. Was this a sign of his lack of interest in clothes or was he just enjoying the contrast with his more usual formal dress?

Segura greeted Constancia by bowing his head slightly instead of the more typical Spanish greeting among friends, a kiss on both cheeks, as he did with Katherine. Then he approached me. Surely he would not greet me with a kiss! I rose from my chair to avoid that and bowed. I sat again, relieved at the informality of our greeting. He and Luis Eduardo got their breakfasts.

The Cardinal sat down at the table next to me, crossed himself, and said to me directly: "Not Low Church I hope?"

I was impressed that he knew the difference between Anglican High Church pretentions at Oxford and the Evangelical Low Church movement at Cambridge. "I was an Irish Catholic," I told him, "educated by the Jesuits in Dublin before going to Cambridge."

"I suppose that explains your good Spanish," he said.

"Well, your Eminence, calling my Spanish 'good' is generous. But, yes, I started studying Spanish in Dublin, and continued at Cambridge. I always wanted to live abroad, and Spain seemed to me an exotic place not all that far away."

"Oh, you think us exotic, do you? I can see how one might, what with Europe's confusion about Spanish mysticism and our backwardness. You know, I suppose, that we have fewer miles of railroads than any country in Europe, and foreigners own a lot of our industry."

Constancia followed the Cardinal's remarks with an ironic smile. "Pedro, you are right about our mysticism and backwardness. Will that ever change with the church so certain of its prerogatives?"

The Cardinal shot Constancia a stern look but again took up his subject, looking at me. "Our backwardness comes from never really recovering our national footing after Philip II tried to invade England in the fifteenth to convert Elizabeth to Catholicism. You call that 'The Spanish Armada,' and we call it 'The Last Of The Great Religious Wars' fought by Spain for the two hundred years before. Are you interested in history from a Spanish perspective or do you subscribe to the north-of-the Pyrenees view of Spain, putting us into a box of religious fanaticism, poverty, and illiteracy, always aggravated by disdain for our tradition of the bullfight? Foreigners think of it as a brutalizing sport, but for us it is a ritual about the triumph of man over animal instincts, of good over evil.

"Spain does not take suffering and death lightly. It permeates our whole culture, like some dark inheritance from the Moors. I am an aficionado of deep Gypsy singing, called *canto jondo*, which for me is like the chanting at mass, a reminder of our immense tolerance of suffering and death. St. Teresa could only have been Spanish, in the way that Freud could only be Viennese."

I was bedazzled that this great man would talk to me in this informal way. I recalled Baedeker emphasizing the innate dignity of Spanish people. There also seemed to be something distinctly Spanish in meeting people on their own terms and letting the chips fall where they may. I stammered out something in Spanish about how what I knew about Spain before coming here was already being challenged by my experiences.

"What did you know about Spain before coming here?" asked the Cardinal.

"Well, your Eminence, for starters, my being able to talk with you is something that I could not imagine happening in Ireland or England, where ecclesiastical haughtiness is severe, not to say patronizing."

The Cardinal smiled at that. "You have another thing coming if you imagine that we Spanish clerics do not cultivate aloofness from each other as well as from our flocks. I come here on weekends to get away from all that, and am grateful to Luis Eduardo and Katherine for allowing me to impose so often on their hospitality. They tell me to come whenever I can, and keep a room just for me. Imagine, an old man who is barely a relative being so welcomed, and one with political views decidedly at odds with my hosts and most of their guests! These visits let me be myself rather than the 'Representative of Rome In Spain,' with all the grandiosity that title implies. I do take that role seriously, mind you, but I also like to be away from it. Perhaps you would like to read a pastoral letter that has got a lot of people's backs up."

"It may surprise you to know that Senora de la Mora told me about your letter just this morning before you came in. I would be honored to read it."

"So, my dear Constancia, thank you for throwing our young Irish gentleman into the deep end of our political debates. My letter had caused my fellow churchmen great consternation, and from what I hear the government has noticed it, and I will be glad to give you a copy. But I must tell you that the negative attention it has generated is a tempest in a teapot. It merely reiterates truths that have long been accepted in Spain. The church's responsibility for educating our young people, for example, is now being criticized as being hidebound by Catholic dogma, and will be replaced by a secular system and the construction of thousands of new schools, the training of secular teachers, and a new curriculum. And what is one to make of women voting, the closing of convents and monasteries, dispersal to peasants of unused privately owned land, and a long list of other "modernizations" that Spain will never support? I expect to remain ostracized by my fellow clerics who seem to think that their silence will carry the day."

"Mr. Fitzgerald may be able to handle these changes better that most Spaniards because he is only an observer, isn't he?" Sra. de la Mora responded. "We have to try to understand what these changes might mean for our futures. You may think I am offended by your conservative views, your Eminence, but I am grateful that we know each other. You tolerate me as best you can, a sign of your good Spanish manners, something that I hope Mr. Fitzgerald notices."

For a moment I did not know what to say. Was I actually expected to comment on Spanish life? I decided that I was. I said, "Your Eminence,

I have only been in Spain for a week but what I was led to believe about Spain has been upended."

"Oh, really? Tell me about that."

"My Baedekers Guide is my main source for information and it has gotten a lot wrong, especially about the food here, which I think is splendid, but which Baedeker seems to think is life-threatening. I read European history at Cambridge but by and large the information we got about Spain stops at 1800, when the Cadiz Constitution was adopted, then promptly rejected by the king. After that, the information about the dynastic wars was very confusing, about which I remember very little. What I know about Spain's current political situation comes from the British press, which seems to fear that your new government will be like the Bolsheviks in Russia."

"Good heavens, a foreigner who knows about the Cadiz experiment! Then you know that Cadiz spawned the short-lived First Republic, which now has been succeeded, 120 years later, by the Second Republic after a sham election. Elections in Spain have never been what Europe calls 'democratic' and this last one was no exception. Democracy will never take hold in Spain. We have had anarchists roaming Catalonia and Andalusia for years, convincing the peasants and industrial workers that their time will only come after the landowners, industrialists, and aristocrats are killed, to say nothing about nuns and priests. So perhaps Europe's assumptions about out political future are more correct that you think."

By this time I was exhausted from trying to follow this complicated conversation in Spanish. But I was also proud to have been able to hold my own in a conversation with this great man. Luis Eduardo had been following the conversation with interest, and now rose from his chair to say that he and I were going to ramble around the countryside and into the village on horseback.

I stood and bowed to the Cardinal, a gesture that he clearly appreciated. He nodded back, smiled, and wished me a pleasant morning.

As Luis Eduardo and I left, Katherine joined us, reminding him that the new schoolteacher was arriving at Granada by train that afternoon from Madrid after his visit with his family in Gijon, and that she would go to Granada with Beltran to collect him. Luis Eduardo told her that we would be back in the late afternoon.

"Can you ride a horse, Mr. Fitzgerald?" Luis Eduardo asked as we left the house.

"Barely."

"Beltran will take care of that, starting tomorrow. " I wondered who Beltran was.

CHAPTER FOUR

Spanish Country Life

O n the way to the stables, Luis Eduardo commented, "If you ride in clothes like you're wearing now, it's hardly surprising that you don't ride well. I will send you to my tailor in Granada, who will make you proper riding clothes, and get you a good pair of riding boots. I will do the same for the schoolmaster. He glanced my corduroy trousers and boots saying, "It gets hot here, so you will also need summer clothes." Luis Eduardo's gesture was generous and helpful without being condescending. I appreciated that.

When we got to the stables, he introduced me to Beltran, the farm manager and, evidently, a good friend of his. He was more than a little put off at the way I was dressed, which Luis Eduardo noticed. "Edwin doesn't yet have a riding costume, but in the meantime, he will wear the spare riding clothes kept for guests."

Beltran seemed mollified that Luis Eduardo had anticipated the problem and shook hands with me before going to prepare the horses we would ride.

The stables were old wooden buildings in good condition. Box stalls were occupied by several horses, mostly Arabians. There was storage for straw, along with other farm paraphernalia, including a four-wheeled carriage, a wagon with seats for transporting guests on outings around the estate, an old fashioned yellow Landau, as well as several motor vehicles: a four-door Ford car, an enormous white car with a black leather top that opened, one windshield for the front seat and another for the back. Luis Eduardo noticed me eying the vehicles and said that his grandfather bought the Landau, and his father owned the white car. Both vehicles were used to transport the family to the Feria in Seville during Easter Week. The Feria had a famous procession of statues of saints carried solemnly through the oldest parts of the city, bullfights, flamenco music, and promenades of ladies and gentlemen in traditional clothes on horseback. The people in the streets carefully observed the riders and applauded when they showed impeccable form.

Luis Eduardo looked at me seriously. "I want you to ride with us next year alongside the yellow carriage, something that will take a lot of work on your part to be able to ride well enough." Luis Eduardo emphasized that horsemanship was an essential skill for someone living on a Spanish farm, and I was to rely on Beltran as my teacher. The prospect of joining Luis Eduardo on horseback at the Feria was a great motivation to take Beltran's training seriously. I thanked him.

Beltran brought out two saddled horses, one a big Spanish Arabian with a beautiful chestnut coat, of which Luis Eduardo took charge. Beltran led the other horse to me, a docile Irish Connemara with a grey and white coat. Beltran put my foot into his hands and boosted me up. The horse was skittish at first, obviously aware that I was an inexperienced rider, but I managed to keep her relatively quiet until we left.

We walked our horses down the entrance drive, under the shade of the Oleander trees, past the pumping station that brought water for the gardens and to generate electricity from a river some miles away, past the ménage with its battered turf and fences for jumping, and, finally, past the schoolhouse and the schoolteacher's cottage.

Luis Eduardo told me that he depended on Beltran to manage the estate, and that they were the same age, both having been born at Los Olivares in 1891. They were inseparable as they grew up. Their life was idyllic, he said, riding ponies in the countryside, their favorite dogs barking at their heels, with a farm hand riding alongside to ensure that they did not get lost. Luis Eduardo was sent to a boarding school when he was ten. But they spent time together during holidays and in the summer, growing into manhood together.

When Don Carlos retired to Madrid, he turned over the management of Los Olivares to Luis Eduardo. Don Carlos joined many of his friends there, enjoying their old age by meeting at cafes for their regular *tertulias*, always at the same cafe for discussions about issues of the day.

We rode slowly through the gently rolling hills of the olive groves, as Luis Eduardo talked about life at Los Olivares. It was hot; insects buzzed around us; the soil was dry, the color of the desert; the air was full of dust and almost concealed the sun. As we got to the crest of a hill, I was astonished by the endless vista of olive trees shimmering in the heat. Tillers had been pulled between the trees leaving long sensual waves of earth between the enormous trees. We stopped once or twice to take in the great gnarled branches covered with gray-green leaves providing shade, riding slowly until we came to the farm road that led us toward the village.

Just outside the village was a cluster of small, dilapidated houses. Open doors were hung with a blue cloth that Luis Eduardo told me the locals believed kept out flies. The thatched roofs were deteriorating. Luis Eduardo said these were the sorts of hovels that Katherine intended to replace with new cottages.

Luis Eduardo nodded to some of the men who were walking in from the fields. They lifted their hats and bowed deeply in response to his greeting. He nodded back, calling out some of the men's names, which appeared to please them.

He stopped and stood in his stirrups, raising himself from his saddle for a moment. "This is Mr. Fitzgerald, from England, who will be staying with us for some time," he told them, "You will see him now and then riding through the countryside or in the village. Please give him the same respect that you give to me." I bowed my head, as Luis Eduard had done, and they nodded in return.

We dismounted at the edge of the village. Luis Eduardo gave the horse's reins to two boys dressed in rags. He bent down, looked the boys directly, and asked them their names. They paused, in awe of talking to Luis Eduardo. One said he was called Lorenzo, and that his family name was Alvarez. The other boy said that he was called Roberto de la Cruz, and that his father was dead, but that his mother was called Carmen Vassalo. Luis Eduardo shook their hands rather formally as they bowed their heads in respect. Luis Eduardo asked each boy to hold the reins of one of the horses and gave each one a coin at which they stared at in amazement. The boys flashed smiles, followed by deep bows and thanks while holding tightly to the reins of our horses. Other children approached the boys, anxious to have a look at their friends' riches.

We walked to a formal plaza paved in stone. There was a tavern called *El Ventrilo Anciano* (The Old Window-Sill) in a whitewashed stone building. A dilapidated Romanesque church stood between the stone building that housed the Guardia Civil and the town hall. Several houses faced the plaza, but most were along narrow streets with water-tracks down the middle.

At the center of the plaza were black painted wooden benches, back to back, which Luis Eduardo told me were used on Sunday evenings during the *paseo*, when young men strolled purposefully up and down in one direction, and girls giggled in groups walking the other way. People would carefully watch this traditional ritual of flirtation, ensuring that there would be no violations of decency.

We stopped for a drink at the tavern, ordering red wine, which was served with a tiny plate of olives. We sat outside on rough stools next to dilapidated wood tables. While we were sitting there an old woman approached us, bowing deeply, murmuring to herself. Luis Eduardo stood up and asked her to sit with us. She declined but told Luis Eduardo that many years ago, when his dear mother, Dona Luisa, opened her school, the woman's daughter, Encarnacion, was one of the first students. She learned to read, to write, and to do sums. Dona Luisa noticed Encarnacion and loaned her books from her own house. She read them - novels she called them - stories about people who lived long ago. Then, in her kindness, Dona Luisa arranged for her daughter to work at the house of one of her friends in Madrid. Her mistress took Encarnacion to Paris and London as her maid. She now lived in Madrid and was content.

The old lady took hold of Luis Eduardo's hand and kissed it. "Thank you, my son, for being the child of such a great lady. We old people in the village worshipped her. Do you remember when you would come with her at Christmas to bring baskets of food, with salt and rice, jars of saffron and sweet nougat with almonds? I still have the blue silk ribbons she gave my daughter and have tied them around the backs of chairs."

Luis Eduardo thanked the old lady for remembering his mother. She bowed modestly and slowly walked away, her head held high, fanning herself with an old black fan.

"I will send her a new fan and some bread and wine." He looked at me. "Now you have seen something of the dignity of the poorest people in Spain, although you also may feel yourself back in some long-dead Europe, or Gogol's vanished Russia.

After a few minutes, an old man with a drum and trumpet walked grandly to the center of the square. He greeted Luis Eduardo with a flourish, and then stood on the steps of the church, where he announced that the Mayor was calling a village-meeting for that evening at 9 pm, at which time he would read "important directives" from the new government in Madrid. It was touching to see the town crier, pompous in his shabby official uniform, all gold piping and crested buttons, turning his announcement into something grandiose. Luis Eduardo told me that to avoid listening to the Mayor, the men would leave the village. Their wives would stand in the main plaza as the mayor read his notice from the steps of the church.

Then he took me to the church. On the wall near the main door, just below the coat-of-arms of the Cardinal Archbishop at Seville, was a yellowing poster dated 1924, in a dusty black frame under glass. It read:

The Twelve Sacred Rules To Govern Local Life.

1. Women shall not appear on the street with dresses that are too tight.
2. They must never wear dresses that are too short.
3. They must be particularly careful not to wear dresses that are too low cut in front.
4. It is shameful for women to walk in the streets with short sleeves.
5. Every woman who appears on the streets must wear stockings.
6. Women must not wear network cloth over parts of the body that must be covered.
7. At twelve, girls must wear dresses that reach to the knee and stockings at all times.
8. Little boys must not appear in the streets with their upper legs bare.
9. Girls must not walk in out-of-the-way places; to do so is both immoral and dangerous.
10. No decent woman or girl is ever seen on a bicycle.
11. No decent woman or girl is ever seen wearing trousers.
12. What they call in the cities "modern dancing" is strictly forbidden.

Luis Eduardo told me that Msgr. Alberto, the local priest, enforced these edicts and would visit transgressors to remind them of the rules. Deviations were mortal sins, requiring confession and penance for forgiveness. I never saw women dressed in ways that violated these rules, although he said that Spanish men viewed these directives with contempt, and occasionally tore down the notices.

CHAPTER FIVE

The New Schoolteacher

It was late afternoon by the time we walked our horses up the driveway to the house. Katherine was standing at the door and introduced Manuel Montilla, the schoolteacher. He was tall, his hair black and curly as a spaniel's. His face was pale, his eyes light blue, his hands had long fingers, and his nails were manicured. His black suit was a little shabby, as was his starched white shirt. There was something serious about him; he did not use expansive gestures when he talked. As a stable boy led the horses away, Manuel hardly moved as Luis Eduardo and I chatted with Katherine. She asked us to join her on the loggia at the back of the house.

As we got to the loggia. Manuel commented on the lawn and asked if it stayed so green because the big trees along the perimeter shaded it. "Yes," Katherine told him, "that and the ancient Arabic water channels that Luis Eduardo's father restored to provide a steady source of water to keep the lawn from browning-out and the flower beds moist during our hot summers. My father-in-law sometimes visits gardens in England, and this is his attempt to have an English garden here. We also have a greenhouse for starting plants to be transplanted outside in the spring. I act as the gardener, with help from the stable boys."

I said that I would like to help in the garden, something that I enjoyed doing for my father in Dublin.

Manuel looked a little intimidated by all this garden talk. "My family has never had a garden because we live in an apartment, but I would like to help out if someone will coach me on what to do." That seemed a generous thing to say.

I smiled at him and said, "I can do that for you." We shook hands on it.

We all sat down on the loggia and Katherine spoke about how much she appreciated me, and now Manuel, coming to Los Olivares to raise the educational standards at her school. She told us that her deceased mother-in-law, Dona Luisa - at which point she and Manuel crossed themselves - had started the school because there were no schools for miles around, and local children would otherwise have no schooling at all. For that reason, and despite its secular sponsorship, the authorities allowed the school to exist but insisted on weekly visits from the local priest to give religious instruction until the students were ten years old. There were lessons between November and March when there was little farm work. The children were given breakfast and at the end of the day were given food to take home.

She said that Spanish education was under the jurisdiction of the Catholic Church. Faith in God and His mercies were what peasants were taught. Reading and writing were a low priority, skills that were thought to distract from learning about faith, morals, and religious myths. Then she said firmly that failing to give children a good education made us no better than parents in primitive societies, who sold their children into slavery.

"When I took over the school several years ago I decided to find a properly educated teacher and found the two of you. Tomorrow I want to show you the curriculum I want to use. It is adapted from *El Institution Libre de Ensenanza* (The Free School of Education) which Manuel attended. Shall we meet at ten in the dining room?"

At that, we all stood up and shook hands. As she left, Katherine said, "Perhaps the two of you could spend some time this afternoon getting to know each other."

I suggested we adjourn to the little white-painted summerhouse at the bottom of the garden. There were no footpaths, just grass to walk on in the traditional English way. It was a fine summer evening, the afternoon light fading into its long farewell to the day, the freshly mown grass filling the air with its sweet smell of the countryside. The teahouse had an elaborate cut-out wood cornice and low, latticed walls separating the little building from the lawn.

As we settled into wicker chairs, I said, "I am very glad to meet you. Dona Katherine told me about you when I arrived last week."

"It is an honor for me to be invited to teach here," Manuel said, "There was a fuss at the Education Department in Madrid about my appointment because they regarded me as too highly educated to be able to teach illiterate peasants in such a remote place."

"From the conversation at dinner last night I am led to believe that the *residencia* where you stayed, is notorious in some way. Do you think that's true?"

"No, it is not, but many people think that. My *residencia* was full of interesting faculty and students, a sort of boiling pot of new ideas. The lecturers were from all over the world, including H. G. Wells and an interesting French architect named Le Corbusier. The people who think us radical are frightened by ideas and behavior that they have not known all their lives. I was happy living there, basking in its reputation for eccentricity and intellectuality, all the while knowing that it was just a place for people who wanted to know about new things. During the summer the school organized travel abroad, and I was in England two years ago, when I visited Cambridge, actually."

I asked Manuel if he would tell me about Spain. "I have only been here for a short time, so, as you might imagine, I know very little about this country."

Manuel thanked me for asking his opinion. "I am afraid that the most important things happening in Spain now are political because of the recent election of a Republican government. For a long time, corruption has been central to political life, as though cash payments for favors, the appointment of relatives to government posts, and the rigging of elections are appropriate ways to operate."

"Spain is divided by mountain ranges, climates, and soil conditions, giving Spaniards a passionately local focus. A man's loyalty is to his village. Individual dignity is paramount, and direct action always just below the surface. Although there is a middle class in the large cities, most of Spain is backward, illiterate, and full of Catholic mysticism and suspicion of intellectual life. Our culture of saying what is on our minds, and damn the consequences, is deeply ingrained. To many Spaniards, patriotism goes no farther than the village, and Spain in the abstract is only a tax collector or a sergeant major of the Guardia Civil.

There is no tradition in Spain of political compromise for the sake of responsible governance."

"As a result, there isn't a shred of democratic tradition to build on. The election of a Republican government last month has increased pressure to resolve long-standing issues, one of which is the distribution to peasants of unused privately owned land. That has been tried many times and always failed. So all of Spain is watching to see if this time will be different. You may know that there have been British investments in Spain since the 16th century, with sherry production at British establishments and the exportation of Spanish oranges from the port of Valencia to Dundee, Scotland, where the famous orange marmalade is produced. So I wonder if Britain is alarmed about our socialist government, and perhaps fears that there isn't much difference between communism and us."

"Yes. The British press is agitated about Spain's new Republican government, with our newspapers reporting ominously about the growth of anarchism and sub-rosa Russian influence. But in Britain the effects of the Great War and the recent depression are still being felt, so I don't think there is any appetite for involvement in Spanish politics. There continues to be resentment that World War I lasted longer than it needed to because Spanish enterprises sold arms and material to all who would pay cash under the smokescreen of political neutrality."

Manuel stood up, lit a cigarette, and said, "You are right that many Spanish enterprises made a great deal of money during the war by selling guns, ammunition, and minerals to anyone who would pay cash. That profits mattered more than human lives will forever be a stain on our national honor. But that wealth did not seep into the public realm, and millions of people suffer from extreme poverty. Time stands still in Andalusia. Unlike the changes in the ways of life on the great plantations in the American South after the Civil War, and on the estates of Russian noblemen after their revolution, the system here is unchallenged and eternal."

He paced back and forth as he smoked, and finally sat down. "Would you mind if I asked why you wanted to come to Spain?"

"Not at all, thank you for asking." I was glad of his interest in my coming to Spain. I told him about wanting to get away from English life, and that my Spanish lecturer at Cambridge knew Luis Eduardo from when he was at school there and arranged for me to come as tutor to his children, so coming to Spain seemed a good opportunity.

"I have had a very middle class upbringing, stuffy and full of rules. My family owns a respectable family business that I have always been expected to join. I did not want to do that, so by the time I finished at Cambridge I was looking for a way to get as far away from Britain as I could, so here I am." Manuel smiled and offered me a cigarette. I smoked, and said to Manuel, "Now it's your turn to please tell me a little about yourself."

"Glad to," he said. "I am from Gijon, in Asturias in the north. My father heads the local branch of the Spanish Socialist Workers Party, which organizes strikes against the owners of coal mines because working conditions are unsafe and the pay is poor. My parents did not want their children educated by nuns or priests, so they sent us to a school called *El Institution Libre de Ensensanza* at Gijon, the secular educational model that Katherine wants to emulate at Los Olivares. I studied philosophy and languages at the University of Madrid, surrounded by lively discussions about politics, art, and life. I should probably call myself an armchair socialist, supportive of change but cautious about the best way to do that.

"I have a particular aversion to the endless number of pointless traditions in Spain. For example, I would think that no other European capital adheres to an inviolate ritual that requires ladies to wear black in the presence of the King at public events. Not mourning clothes, mind you, far from it; beautiful formal clothes that are elegant and flattering, refined. To have courage is to appear in a glamorous short red dress, if courage is the correct word. It's simple to have the courage to not wear black in the presence of the King. Everyone would be appalled, but so what? From what one hears about King Alfonso, he would be delighted. I mean really, if socialism means anything at least it should encourage abandoning the silliest of our traditions, royal and otherwise. I desire a future that breaks the ties of the past."

I loved Manuel's example and said, "But can there ever be an old culture that does not have pointless rules? In Ireland, there is a particularly distasteful tradition of measuring the status of a family by whether they have black clothes for a funeral as a matter of course. There is not enough time between death and the burial to get new wardrobes, so only wealthy people can afford to be equipped with mourning clothes that are ready on short notice."

"And where was your family on that measure of status?"

"We had black clothes made every few years so they'd fit at a moment's notice."

We both laughed. "Something for us to share," Manuel said, "disdain for pointless traditions."

"What about bull-fighting? I am sure you know that what you call a sport is regarded very differently outside Spain. It is surely the only sport where one of the participants is meant to be killed."

"I presume that you have not been to a bullfight."

"No, I have not."

"Good, because they are now mostly commercialized affairs, where one rarely sees the kind of beautiful gestures that are part of a great bullfight. That now only happens in villages, where young bullfighters show their courage and mesmerize the crowd by their daring. I was once at a bullfight in a village outside Madrid. In the sixth and last fight the torero was a young man in a white suit with silver embroidery that sparkled in the late afternoon sun. He led the bull through more and more dangerous passes. Each time the bull's blood was smeared on his outfit, vividly red against his white suit. The atmosphere was electric with anxiety for the bullfighter, the crowd shouting for the performance to end. He finally ended with a kill that was utterly moving, elegant and swift, the magnificent animal falling at the young bullfighters feet as he slowly turned his back and walked away. The crowd silently stood up, the ultimate accolade, followed by a roar of recognition for the bullfighter's bravery. The reputations of such daring young men spread by word of mouth. Eventually, one such bullfighter will appear on a program in a nearby village, and we will go together."

At that, we stopped talking. Manuel got up from his chair and said, "Now, if you will excuse me, I want to go to my cottage and rest for a while. Shall we meet there tonight? My cottage is at the bottom of the entrance drive next to the schoolhouse."

"I would like that," I said. I went to my room, bathed, had my siesta, dressed and then walked down the driveway to Manuel's cottage.

The door was ajar, so I knocked and went in. Manuel thanked me for coming and smiled as he shook my hand, making me feel at ease. He now wore faded black corduroy trousers, raffia sandals, and a wrinkled linen shirt open at the neck. There was a whiff of cologne about him.

His cottage was one of the new ones, like the ones being built for farm workers. The roof was tiled above whitewashed walls, with a door at center flanked by windows. There were a pair of padded armchairs on either side of a fireplace that was nearly big enough to step into, its back and sidewalls barely blackened by fire ash because it had just been built. It contained a cooking apparatus and a grate. A fire was burning quietly. Simple cabinets lined the sidewall with a stone countertop that included a tin sink and a faucet for water that, Manuel told me, came from a barrel on the roof. Shelves held simple crockery and glasses, as well as a few pieces of table linen. There were old wooden chairs next to a small dining table. A ladder led to a loft that I presumed held sleeping quarters. At the back of the room, a glass door opened onto a small paved area with an old wicker chair. Mature trees surrounded the little building, throwing dappled moonlight everywhere.

Each cottage had its own *excusat*, a hole in the ground with sackcloth for a door and bits of paper hanging on a hook. This was a luxury for people so poor they were used to sharing this kind of facility with dozens of their neighbors.

I thanked Manuel, who said that I would always be welcome, and motioned for me to sit in one of the fireside chairs. Without asking if I wanted anything to drink, he poured two glasses of red wine, gave me one, and then sat down next to me. He asked what I thought of Los Olivares. I said that I had been there for such a short time I was just learning about it. Manuel said that Luis Eduardo asked him to visit his tailor in Granada to get summer clothes, riding clothes and boots. I told him that the same invitation had been extended to me.

"I must say that this gesture from Luis Eduardo is surprising, don't you think?" I asked him. "Or is it something that one would expect in our situations?"

"Not at all to be expected," said Manuel. " I do not know how to ride, but Luis Eduardo told me that someone named Beltran would take us under his wing and quickly get us into decent riding form. We are to meet every morning before breakfast at the stables for our lessons, rain or shine."

I told Manuel that I had already gotten my horse but only rode it once when Luis Eduardo and I went to the village.

"Ah, so we will start off on the same footing," he said.

Learning to ride would be a mountain for me to climb. Controlling the horse and getting it to respond to my commands would be hard work, and my success, or not, would be seen by everyone.

I talked about my formative experience with horses, which was during the time my family's horse farm became a rehabilitation center for shell-shocked soldiers after W.W.I. They were undergoing a new kind of therapy which involved interaction with horses: walking them quietly in the paddock, grooming, feeding, haltering and leading them, accompanied by attendants. Patients with their nurses often came outside in fair weather. They often told me about their families and children, and how grateful they were that their therapy changed them from exhausted, wounded men to functioning people, some of whom faced the daunting possibility that they might not be able to walk again.

I was surprised at having been so open about my experience that had happened long ago with wounded soldiers, about which I had never spoken until now. It seemed a good omen that I would trust Manuel, whom I had just met, with this kind of emotional story. Manuel also seemed affected, and we sat quietly for a while.

He changed the subject by saying that he was surprised but pleased to have been invited to join the family for lunch every Sunday, that he intended to be there, and he hoped I would too. I nodded and then asked if he knew that engaging people were invited for long weekends.

"Katherine said something about that, telling me that people would be there that I might not meet anywhere else, although I was not sure what she meant.

I told him about dinner my first day, and how interesting it was to be seated next to Cardinal Segura y Saenz and across from the first woman to be divorced in Spain, Constancia de la Mora. As I spoke I realized how exciting it was for me to be at Los Olivares, learning about a new culture and meeting fascinating people. Manuel smiled broadly as he listened, making me suspect that he was also glad to be there.

We talked about the new curriculum that Katherine expected us to establish at her school. "It is very unusual for a little country school to have academic ambitions," Manuel said. "It will be a challenge for the families of the students to find the time for their children to study at home."

We also talked about *Misiones Pedagogicas*. Manuel said that the first villages to be visited by the program were now being chosen. "If Luis Eduardo would ask for it to come here, it would likely get at the head of the list of locations. What do you think?"

I did not immediately reply. We had just arrived, after all, and to suggest such a thing seemed impertinent, but I was getting used to people saying things that would have been disconcerting to me before I came to Spain.

Manuel noticed my reticence, and so I said, "Well, it is obviously impossible for me to judge whether or not the program should come to Villanueva de Granada. It certainly seems worth a discussion with Katherine but perhaps we should first get the lay of the land about how she decides things. When we talk with Katharine about the coming school term, we could segue into a conversation about *Misiones Pedagogicas* as a teaching tool for the children. We want her to ask us what would need to be done for it actually to happen. Then we will have gotten her into our mousetrap, and can begin talking about logistics.

"She will never fall for that," I admitted.

Manuel laughed. "Of course not, at first, but in Spain, where people are very straightforward with each other, being indirect is sometimes good." I was impressed with Manuel's strategic skills.

"Do you know about Katherine's photographic project?" I asked.

"No," he said.

"She told me that she intends to take portrait photographs of each person in each family in the village and then give them each a copy in a simple black wood frame behind glass. She is a devotee of August Sander, a German photographer who has photographed thousands of ordinary Germans, believing that people's status, even their professions, can be indicated by their clothes and how they hold themselves."

"Manuel said that peasants would be very grateful to have a photograph of themselves and their family, framed and behind glass. They probably see it as no more than a kindness from Dona Katherine. But showing images of peasants as individuals, rather than a class of serfs to be exploited, will not be appreciated by the district's powers-that-be."

I began to wonder if Katherine's photographic project was as much a political gesture as an artistic event.

As I was leaving we stopped to look at the school building, which was next to Manuel's house It was a one room structure plastered inside and out and painted white, with bright blue window frames. There was a blackboard with chalk, chairs with little tabletops, and a larger desk for the teacher at the head of the room on a platform. Shelves were stocked with notebooks and supplies. Each side wall had two windows with shutters on the inside against drafts, which were painted a lighter shade of blue. The wood floor was polished to a dull sheen. There were coat hooks between the windows and a big metal stove. The little room breathed the deep warmth of a building that had never been cold, something unknown to the peasants whose hovels were cold all winter. The twigs and sticks that Luis Eduardo allowed to be gathered were never enough to keep them warm.

Katherine told Manuel that the building was kept in good condition by the men and the families of the students, who wanted their schoolhouse neat and trim. It was their gesture of thanks for the education of their children, and, as important, for feeding them during the day and sending food home.

When leaving the schoolhouse, I bid farewell, and walked up the driveway to the house, very glad that Manuel and I had so quickly become comfortable talking about ourselves and our families.

CHAPTER SIX

Augustin Beltran, Spanish farmer

One of the people I first got to know well, apart from Manuel, was Augustin Beltran, the farm manager. He was an austere figure with a withered face, his eyes dark as linseed. Every morning at first light, before our riding lessons, he walked purposely around the estate inspecting the stables and giving instructions to farm workers.

Whenever I saw him, he wore the same kit: black rubber Wellington boots, dark-colored corduroy trousers tucked into them, a shabby waxed cotton jacket in a sort of dirty-green color, a fine white cotton shirt, and a black wide brimmed hat, well brushed and perfectly suited to his noble head. Around his neck, there was a dark-colored scarf, knotted at the throat and tucked into his shirt.

Luis Eduardo told me that Beltran was to be treated with deference. It was easy for me to do that; he had chosen a horse that was to become mine during my stay, and he would become our instructor in the proper Spanish way of riding.

"Not wearing an appropriate costume of riding is no small matter," Beltran told me. "Otherwise, your horse will not understand your commands, and you would only be able to ride donkeys."

Beltran urged me to become demonstrative, as it would help my horse understand my instructions. I hoped that learning to ride might also help me overcome my shyness, something incomprehensible to anyone brought up in Spain. To be shy in England is testament to having been well brought up, where it was understood that an Englishman was never so natural as when he was holding his tongue. Spaniards did not seem to appreciate the quality of the English reaction to a direct question, which was invariably one of suspicion and reticence. In Spain being modest and quiet generated pitying looks.

Beltran's respect for status made him quiet when he was around me, although he often looked at me with that prolonged Spanish stare, as though to exorcise my shyness. I did change, to a degree, becoming more talkative with greater ease. Beltran noticed and would give me a sly smile, as if to say, "Perhaps there is hope for our young Englishman after all."

My admiration for Beltran, and our increasing ease in each other's presence, led to a surprising turn. As my horse was being saddled one morning, Beltran asked me about Manuel. Beltran's interest in the school was of a piece with his other work at the farm: earnest, dutiful.

He asked me if the new teacher knew anything about the lives of his students. I said that I was only just getting to know him, but was impressed with his commitment to the education of the children at the village school and his enthusiasm for new ways of teaching them.

"What do you mean by new ways?" Beltran said evenly. "Isn't the new teacher too highly educated for us?"

"Yes, he is highly educated," I said, "and lived at a distinguished *Residencia* where he heard lectures from some of the most advanced scientists, artists, philosophers and politicians in Europe."

"Ah, Europe," he said gravely, "Europe is always dangerous for Spain. France is in Europe, and France had Napoleon, who invaded Spain, replacing our Charles IV with his brother, Joseph. France ruins everything." I looked at him admiringly.

"What makes you stare at me like that?" he asked.

"How would you know that?"

"I know people who tell me things that I need to know," he replied.

'What sort of people, and what need is there for you to know Spanish history"?

"Just people," he said as he lifted my left foot to get me in my saddle and tightened the straps under the horse's belly, smacking my horse on its rump to get it moving.

The next afternoon Manuel and I were sitting in the summerhouse talking about whether there was a way to get the students involved with welcoming *Misiones Pedagogicas* to the village when Beltran walked across the lawn toward us. We stopped talking, stood up, and shook his hand, surprised by his visit.

We sat down as Beltran leaned against the railing, lit a cigarette, and asked: "Do you want to know about the peasant life in this part of Spain?" His voice was flat, holding much in reserve, a voice that guarded its secrets, the sort of Spaniard who preserved the sense of individuality and the distinct personality that was being lost in modern times.

Manuel and I glanced at each other. He noticed that and was somehow offended and turned to leave.

"Please stay and talk with us," I said. "Unless we know about the lives of our students and their families, we cannot succeed, Don Agustin."

"I am not Don Augustin, and you must not call me that. I am Beltran. You, our young Irishman, have been here long enough to notice that I am to be addressed by my name, just my name. How could you have missed that, with your education and your life amongst grand people? My wife is Consolata. We are nothing more than that. At our death, we will be dust, ashes, nothing. When Don Luis Eduardo dies, there will be a tomb, and his heirs will light candles for the salvation of his eternal soul."

We were a little shaken by Beltran's harshness.

"What else have you not noticed? If I told it to you about our life here, what would you understand about that? How can I be sure that you are genuinely interested in our young people? How can I know that what you call 'new ideas' will be good for them?"

Beltran looked at us skeptically. Finally, he sat down but apart from us on a bench. "It is clear to me that neither of you ever lived in the middle of nowhere, as you are now. Why do you want to live amongst us when you can have a pleasant life amongst people like yourselves? Would it surprise you to realize that it is dangerous for me, and for other workers, to talk to outsiders?" Beltran asked Manuel to loan him a cigarette, "until next Thursday." Then he slowly walked away.

Beltran came to see us a few days later when we were again in the summerhouse. But this time he spoke as though he had worked out in advance what he wanted to say. It was clear this was not to be a conversation between equals.

Beltran started by telling us the words of an old Andalusia song:

This drum is just like you
It makes a loud noise
But look inside---it is empty.

"Think about that, as we talk. One of us may turn out to be the drum, and one may be the noise. Perhaps we both will be both. Listen carefully to me now, and I will tell you things. Have you ever heard of Anarchism?"

"Yes, I know what that is," said Manuel. I was not so sure I did.

Beltran told us that for years itinerant Anarchists had been in Andalusia. Wherever they went, they organized clandestine political meetings. Strangers were always suspect, so they never stayed for long. Anarchists preached that everyone should have what they needed as a matter of right, not have to beg for every crumb, that the powers-that-be wanted the great political silence to continue. The changes being proposed by the new government seemed to peasants an opening to destroy conventional ways of life, to assert their rights. They wanted revenge.

"This is a region of huge estates and wretchedly paid labor. The olive groves cover the hills for mile after mile, and in the midst of such wealth it is hard to accept our grinding poverty. Andalusia is a region of serfdom, the Spanish Russia. People here manage to live even though they are reduced to forced labor, controlled by the bailiffs, kept down, and when they protest, beaten by the Civil Guard. Everyone is aware of the enormous gap between the extreme poverty of the villagers and what must be the huge profits generated by the olive groves. Anarchism thrives in this environment, breeding revolt against the landlords, who have no interest in and little information about their peasants since they rarely visited their estates. When they do, they have to be accompanied by the Guardia Civil for their safety.

"We say to each other: When one eats well, good. When one eats badly, that is not so good. It is the most constant Spanish saying amongst peasants. We are always brought down to the fundamentals of life; my parents are dead; my parents are alive; life is sad; life is gay. Our lives show us primitive good and evil. We remain living until we are put into the ground. Then nothing. Nothing. No people in Spain are more gracious, none poorer than the peasants of Andalusia. There is great poverty here but somehow no squalor. Why can others spend all day sitting doing nothing in a cafe in Granada, or lie in bed all day in Madrid, to get up and talk and play cards with friends all night?

"Sooner or later you will run across a group of fine fellows, naked to the waist, putting down their pick-axes, rushing at you, wanting to talk. They will take off their hats. "Why do you come here? To look at our misery? Do people eat well in your country? Here we starve. How can one keep a wife and children on a few pesetas a day?

"Then you will know about Spanish manners. Amid all their servitude, they do not whine or threaten. In their excitability, they do not lose their human dignity or good manners. Mothers here are forced to beg for food to give their helpless infants, who, as they grow up, often turn to thievery for want of work. Spanish peasants cannot read, and there are almost no schools to teach them. They are dimly aware that there is Madrid, but know it never produces anything useful."

He stopped there, energized by his passionate speech. Manuel and I sat in astonishment, deeply moved. As he walked away, he stopped, turned, and said quietly, "It is best to begin friendship with a little aversion."

Discussions about bringing *Misiones Pedagogicas* to Villanueva de Granada were taking on a new coloration for me. Were we contemplating a project that could have consequences beyond the intentions of the program? Or was I floundering in complicated information for which I had no background?

CHAPTER SEVEN
Katherine's Photographs

One morning Katherine asked Manuel and me to come to her studio to look at her photographs. We hoped that Katherine would support the possibility of *Misiones Pedagogicas* coming to Villaneuva de Granada and were excited at the prospects of what could come of the studio visit.

We met at the door to the main house and walked to the studio through a grove of birch trees on a carpet of wild grass, following a stone footpath. There were laurustines, southern European evergreen shrubs, and masses of viburnum with large clusters of white and pink flowers. We sat on wicker chairs in a little paved area next to the studio. Consolata appeared with tea, which she left on a table next to Katherine, who poured as we sat enjoying the warm sun.

"When I first got here," she said, "I wanted to fit in as fast as possible and was glad when Begonia introduced me to the Spanish tradition of wealthy women doing good works. Our 'good work' was to win over the parish priest from his suspected liberal views. That meant visiting the local priest in Begonia's immense car, and offering to buy altar wine and candles. We did not bother to tell the parish priest that we were coming, so he was surprised to see us. He wore a weather-beaten cassock turned the color of fly's wings, soiled and without buttons, and he had not shaved for days. The Church was in bad condition: dirty, bare, and decrepit. My stepmother-in-law promised the priest a new carpet and other needed decorations. When we left she said smugly that he would never again vote against the conservatives.

"On the way back to Los Olivares we passed through the village. Seeing a tumbledown pile of stones and mud inhabited by peasants, I cried out, 'People can't be living here!' And I decided then and there to do something about this shocking situation, which led to my project of building of cottages for the peasants who worked in the fields and olive orchards, and then hiring you both to improve the education at our school.

"My husband was taken aback by my intentions. He had been raised here and knew very well the intractability of peasant life. And yet, when the first of the new peasant houses was nearly complete, Luis Eduardo seemed proud that I had prevailed."

Katherine said she hoped that she had begun something that could be an example of what the local landowners could do to improve the lives of their peasants, but Luis Eduardo said that local landlords would have no interest in doing anything that would reduce their profits, and certainly would not build new cottages for their peasants!

I was impressed by Katherine's candor at saying all this to us. Although she and I were both the products of the British middle class, she had become comfortable with the Spanish way of being straight-forward and speaking her mind without kowtowing and hedging her bets. I admired her for that!

Katherine's studio was a one story stone building with a slate roof, and big windows closed by shudders on the outside. She said the studio had only been visited by the people she photographed, her husband, and now us.

When we went inside, Katherine said that the inspiration for her photographic project at Los Olivares sprang from an exhibition that she and Luis Eduardo had seen in Cologne with photographs by August Sander, a German photographer, when they were traveling in Germany in 1929. She showed us the exhibition catalogue, entitled *Face of Our Time: Faces, Pictures And Their Truth* containing hundreds of Sander's black and white photographs. Sander called them a "Portfolio of Archetypes." The sitters were identified, not by name, but by occupation or type: from land workers to factory workers, to artistic and professional elites, to the frail and the elderly, with a respectful and unadorned neutrality, and always within their familiar surroundings. They posed in various ways: walking as a group or sitting for an individual or family portrait. There was an eerie monumentality about the subjects.

I especially admired "Odd Job Man," of a young bricklayer balancing a stack of bricks on his shoulders, and another entitled "Young Farmers," of three men standing on a rural footpath wearing dark suits, white shirts, and ties, wide-brimmed hats set at rakish angles, looking backwards over their right shoulders while leaning on their walking sticks.

Katherine's goal was to highlight her subject's dignity, human-ity, and, in the process, to make a connection with the egalitarian expectations being fostered by the new Republican government. She said that it was more likely that her photographs would be seen by the local establishment as an unwelcome assumption that the peasants are individuals, not merely part of a faceless mob.

Manuel said that *Misiones Pedagogicas* "will introduce peasants to a larger world, and to ideas about change that may be coming."

Katherine listened carefully. "I am glad you brought up *Misiones Pedagogicas*. I have already talked with Luis Eduardo about it, and he will visit the appropriate officials in Madrid to formally request that our village be one of the first for the program to visit."

Manuel smiled slightly as he declared portentously, "Dona Katherine, this is good news. I will be glad to help. Edwin, what do you think?"

I replied earnestly, "I will do whatever I can to help." I looked at my friend, Manuel, admiring his audacity for asking Katherine about *Misiones Pedagogicas*, and glad at her reply.

The studio was a large bright room with shelves for bottles of printing fluids, cabinets of small drawers that stored photographic paper and the final prints, a large worktable, a few chairs, and a small cast iron stove. There was also a small room containing a sink for rinsing the prints with a bare red bulb and strings crisscrossing the ceiling to hold the photographs as they dried.

We put on white cotton gloves as Katherine opened drawers containing the photographs. She took some of them out and put them on the large table. We used magnifying loupes to look closely at the pictures. Manuel asked if it was hard to get people to agree to be photographed. She replied that many asked their confessor. Some were discouraged by Msgr. Don Alberto, who replied that having photos of themselves was vain, a form of idolatry, and that no one should participate. But most were curious about the prospect of being photographed by the mistress of the estate and elated that they would get framed portraits to put on their walls.

Katherine wondered how the powers-that-be would react if indeed they allowed themselves to think about a peasant's right to be perceived as an individual. "And wasn't *Misiones Pedagogicas* going to help all of us, peasants included, to see things in a new way? Challenging assumptions of the powers-that-be was the point, wasn't it?"

"Luis Eduardo is alert to the political implications of showing my photographs, but that intrigues him because it's a way to exert his political power and status as the scion of a local aristocratic family. Begonia will be apoplectic at the idea of her foreign stepdaughter-in-law exhibiting these photographs on a property owned by her husband's family, and will do whatever she can to stop it. Since that is likely to fail, she will work hard to make the visit unsuccessful."

"Can Begonia's opposition be managed?" I asked Katherine. She thought for a moment, sat down, and asked us to do the same saying forcefully, "As you have noticed, Begonia is full of the air of always knowing best. She believes in the infinite vulgarity of newness and is determined to remain unspoiled by it. She devotes herself to the old, the consecrated, with immense esteem for tradition, the set of beliefs of her generation and her class. She is like a serpent in a bank of flowers, disguised but ready to pounce at the slightest opportunity."

Although I had grown to like Begonia in some way, she was absurdly preoccupied with her status. Once I observed her as she was getting up from lunch holding a glass of red wine. She dropped it to the floor, shattering the glass and spilling wine onto the carpet. She sat down acting as if nothing had happened until she looked at Katherine condescendingly and said, "Go find someone to clean this up. One cannot expect a Spanish aristocrat to bend down." She then went slowly out of the room, pausing to shoot me a look of triumph. My being in the room added insult to injury. This incident made me wary around Begonia, but I tried to stay in her good graces. There was always uncertainty about her mood. It was always possible that something might set her off. And she had certainly shown what a Tartar she could be when aroused!

Katherine's candid remarks to Manuel and me were akin to being at dinner with the Cardinal speaking nicely to the first divorced woman in the new socialist Spain. I was suddenly thrilled to be amongst people who related to others in ways entirely new to me.

Manuel spoke first. "Dona Katherine, thank you very much for showing us your work. I think these photographs will be perfectly fitting as part of the visit by *Misiones Pedagogicas*."

A few days later, Katherine told us that she would bring up the visit from *Misiones Pedagogicas* after dinner that night. Manuel and I were invited, but Katherine asked us not to join in unless asked to, as the talk was likely to become heated.

We assembled as usual in the drawing room before dinner. Begonia said gaily, "Poor Ottilie, none of last year's clothes will fit her by Christmas. So I have ordered a winter wardrobe for her that is suitable for a well brought up child. That's what an *abuela* needs to do when her granddaughter is made to dress in shabby trousers, mended shirts, and filthy worn out boots!"

Katherine shot an exasperated look at Begonia. "Please don't go to any trouble. Consolata and my maid can make anything that Ottilie and her brothers need."

Begonia replied with a triumphant smile, saying, "I am the child's grandmother and can give her anything I want." Then she asked me to bring her a glass of wine, which I did.

A man came in to announce dinner. Begonia rose from her chair and, as had become her custom, asked me to take her in, as was her habit now. I always went out of my way to pull Begonia's chair back from the table so she could be seated.

Katherine rang the bell. The first course was clear soup with a pigeon in it. Boiled crayfish was next, followed by grilled lamb with Russian salad, then sliced fruit, and little cookies. Begonia's and Katherine's set-to about the children's clothes made the mood a little tense, so we talked more or less about the weather.

After dinner, we went to the loggia, Begonia, and Katherine chatting as they sat down. Manuel and I stood smoking cigarettes at the edge of the veranda, and Luis Eduardo sat in a comfortable chair, lighting his pipe. Consolata came in with little cakes. Then she stood quietly in the background. Luis Eduardo called for a whiskey and asked Manuel and me if we would like some. We said no.

Katherine said that she wanted to talk about preparations for the visit of *Misiones Pedagogicas*. But first, looking directly at Begonia, she said that she would describe the program itself so everyone could understand what it was. "The new Government in Madrid has created educational missions to visit the most impoverished villages in Spain. Their charge is to spread general culture by setting up a temporary museum to exhibit copies of the great paintings from the Prado, by establishing a village library; organizing a district choral group; and building a makeshift theater to present the great plays of Spain and Europe. Recordings of European classical music and Spanish music will be listened to in the open air. The library and a gasoline-powered electrical generator will be left in the village.

"*Misiones Pedagogicas* visits are managed by teachers, actors, writers, costume designers, painters, and musicians, who work alongside the inhabitants of the villages during their stay. Villanueva de Granada has been chosen to have this program both because it is very poor, and because of our school and its tradition of helping people learn new things. Luis Eduardo and his father have agreed to open their house in the village to accommodate our visitors. The organizers and students would occupy the upstairs bedrooms."

Katherine said that she intended to exhibit her portrait photographs at the family house. She hoped we all agreed that dignified images of people, titled with the jobs they performed, was a way to demonstrate the dignity of all forms of work and to honor people's inherent humanity.

As Katherine was speaking, Begonia stepped to the edge of the loggia, moving her fan vigorously. Then she said forcefully that no circumstances or information could convince her to support this foolishness, declaring that an exhibition of Katherine's photographs was especially wrong-headed. "There is nothing new about governments in Madrid grasping at far-fetched ideas about the future of Spain. But this dissemination of general culture will confuse the peasants at best, and at worst will empower illiterate Spain to think that they can improve their circumstances and contribute to the New Spain." Begonia sat down and stared at Luis Eduardo.

Katherine was not intimidated by Begonia's odious provincial gentility. She said, "I am sure that one of the things that disturbs Begonia is our project to build modest cottages for the families of our workers. I am inspired to do so by my dear father's devotion to the welfare of his

workers at his woolen mills in the north of England. My father would
be proud that the inheritance he left me is being put to good use, and
so am I."

Luis Eduardo put down his pipe. "Thank you, Katherine, for
describing *Misiones Pedagogicas* so clearly, and thank you for mentioning
your project to build cottages for our workers. Thanks also to Begonia
for letting us know her opinion. She is right about Spain's turbulent
political history. During the past fifteen years there have been forty-three
military *pronunciados*, coupes d' etat, actually, each of which established
new governments. In addition, the taint of Spanish anarchism inspired
the assassination of three prime ministers. One of Spain's great failings
has been its inadequate educational system that has been operated by the
Catholic Church as far back as anyone can remember. Spain's illiteracy
rate is 30%, which amounts to 8,000,000 Spaniards out of twenty five
million who cannot read or write. *Misiones Pedagogicas* is one of the
ways to start to expand educational opportunities."

Luis Eduardo picked up a newspaper and said, "I want to read
something by the minister of education, who is also the founder of
Misiones Pedagogicas, from last week's newspaper:

"The Church has stood for the oppression of freedom, putting down
all heterodoxy, and misrepresented the views of those who disagreed with
it. We are not calling for revenge, only for justice. The new Republic must
not repay the Church in its own coin of intolerance. It merged with an
oppressive and dysfunctional monarchy and the financial establishment;
persecuted, burned, and maimed; it expelled the Jews. To the Spanish
people the Church is a racket, pure and simple, a two-thousand-year-
old swindle, inducing human beings to fear where there is nothing to
fear, and hope when there is nothing to hope for."

He continued, "There is growing frustration that the Church has not spoken out in support of the long-needed changes in Spanish life, which indirectly leads to incidents like last Sunday in Madrid, when the monarchist club broadcast into the street a recording of the Royal Anthem. Angry crowds gathered to protest. Civil Guards unable to control the crowd, fired and killed two people. The next day, various groups set fire to churches and convents in the capital. In response to that chaos, the minister of war unwisely remarked, 'All the convents in Madrid are not worth the life of one Republican.' The best minds of an old civilization must double their horsepower to overcome the gravitational field of tradition. Only a few will ever fly."

"I have something else to read, a letter from our friend Cardinal Segura delivered by messenger this morning: 'I am hastily writing to let you know that the socialist government has ordered me expelled from Spain over the Holy Fathers explicit objections. I leave in 48 hours for France. The Prime Minister's telegram to me alluded to my recent pastoral letter objecting to the government's actions, and to my opposition to their diabolical agenda for the future. I will be in touch with you when I get settled. In the meantime, I send my blessings to you and your family.' Signed Pedro Segura y Saenz, Cardinal Archbishop of Toledo and Papal Nuncio to Spain."

Then Luis Eduardo said gravely, "These are the sort of extreme actions that one fears from the new government. Segura's outspokenness is something to be admired and encouraged. But we now can see that the government has limits to its patience with democratic behavior."

There was tense silence until Begonia said with passion: "Such outrageous behavior by the government is frightening to anyone who has hopes for the future of Spain. This defamation of the Catholic Church is nothing new, but I am disappointed to hear it repeated in this house. All Spain needs for a great future is to honor the traditions that have always been the basis of Spain's greatness: the traditional *grandeza* of the Spanish aristocracy: nobleness, graciousness, and generosity. Our priests guide ladies from the best families to priests in poor parishes, who direct us how to help those that they consider 'the deserving poor.' We even give money to the churches in the Madrid districts where people live in self-built shacks without running water or sanitary facilities and we visit these areas ourselves. Even the Queen contributes to our charities."

"I seem to be the only one who is bewildered about what is going on here tonight. Doesn't anyone else in this family understand how dangerous this *Misiones Pedagogicas* is? Peasants have no reason to look at paintings, or listen to foreign music, or watch plays, and worse, to have a library, things that will distract them from their work and encourage them to take on airs about themselves. Attempts at democracy have always failed in Spain, and always will."

Begonia sat down, began to drink her coffee, picked up a little cake, looked at it, and said, "Too sweet," putting it back on the plate, which made a scratching sound as she moved it across the table.

Then it was Katherine's turn. She spoke about the reality of peasant's lives, and how she had come to admire their stamina, their patience, and their anger. She also saw the impact the school had on peasants' lives. "What is education useful for if it is not the first step toward understanding a larger world? Luis Eduardo's mother, Dona Louisa, a great lady from another time, started the village school, as one of those gestures from aristocratic ladies that you speak about, Begonia. *Misiones Pedagogicas* will be an extension of the schoolhouse experience. It will be limited and transient, and will be in Villanueva de Granada only briefly and then move on to another village. This program is important because it honors the capacity of everyone to learn new things and to enlarge their view of the world beyond their village, and trivial at the same time because it will reach so few people. There is nothing to fear," she concluded.

It was like listening to an opening argument for the Rights of Mankind. I was very moved, and from the look on Manuel's face, so was he.

Begonia seemed barely able to contain herself from striking Katherine. "I could never have imagined being made to listen to such ideas in this house. They represent everything I despise and will lead to the destruction of my way of life." She continued grandly, "I know my peasants. My maid is my friend. I confide in her, and I listen to her. When I travel, I give some of my food to peasant children along the journey. I give families money after a death. We do not need to show peasants who they are or could be, any more than they can tell us about ourselves. We are only what we are, now and forever. Everything good in their lives comes from us. Everyone, including the peasants, knows that and accepts it. At school, we were taught to distinguish the deserving poor from the undeserving, and as charitable rich girls, we sold our dolls to give money to the poor, along with food and medicines for the sick. That is the way to help our poor peasants, not to give them new cottages with window glass, and if one can imagine such a thing, having boys and girls in the same classroom!"

Luis Eduardo looked directly at her. "The men of New Spain intend to create a secular system of education that will reduce Spain's shameful illiteracy rate. Our school will remain in operation as a way of augmenting this national program of education and school building.

My mother's intention when she founded our school was to teach our peasant children to read and do sums. Katherine's new curriculum will build on that goal with the help of Manuel and Edwin."

I must have looked agitated because Luis Eduardo said to me, "Edwin, dear boy, you look as if you want to say something."

I was anxious at being put on the spot. But here I was, living amid a family that thrived on a kind of continuous verbal jousting. People talked fast and often at the same time, and the last word was always the most important. I summoned the courage and began. "Thank you, sir, for asking for my opinion. I won't presume to comment on Spanish education, but I can say that the impressions I had about Spain from Baedeker's and British newspapers have been upended by my experience here. The Spain I know is a country of generous people with definite opinions, letting the chips fall where they may, and it's exhilarating to be amongst people who so eloquently express their views. I try to be a person who values integrity, austerity, understatement and a laconic, wry sense of humor."

"But politically, I suppose I am a conservative of sorts growing up believing reactionary phrases that drive people of democratic leanings wild with rage--my station and its duties, the love of personal privacy, of order, of manners, the idea of fairness. I think that these are the virtues that should be used to judge the present and control the future. But even in England, almost nothing in modern life is like that." I sat down and stared at my boots.

Luis Eduardo said, "Thank you for saying kind things about our ways, Edwin." Then he turned to Manuel. "In the spirit of our little Los Olivares Republic, I would like to hear what Manuel has to say."

Manuel stood up, clearly not intimidated by this invitation to speak. Then he gave a speech that astonished me. "Spain is a country where there is a long history of common people against the government. The clergy and aristocracy generates a deep severance of the people from the ruling classes, the bourgeoisie, and the intelligentsia. We obsess over things that do not matter, while being oblivious to things that do matter, always a symptom of an old civilization's disintegration. We seem not to notice that the fat man eating quails while children are begging for bread is a disgusting sight. Poverty is everywhere to be seen-- women aged beyond their years, men misshapen, blind, or mindless. Sometimes the poverty is so primitive that you have to rub your eyes or blink to make sure you are in Europe at all. Is it any wonder that Anarchism flourishes here? In this context, a visit from *Misiones Pedagogicas* will be merely an opening salvo in what is sure to become a great war of ideologies about Spain's future. The program only entails exhibiting paintings, listening to music, people singing in chorales, discussions on how the village people can participate in the New Spain. There is nothing to fear in these activities; they merely help define, as Dona Katherine said so movingly tonight, everyone's basic humanity."

Before Manuel sat down, he went to Luis Eduardo and bowed, then stopped in front of Katherine and Begonia, and bowed again. He sat down next to me, flushed and proud of his eloquence. Even Begonia seemed moved by Manuel's remarks.

Luis Eduardo spoke. "Perhaps we are the victims of our past, unable to imagine that the new government in Madrid can succeed. It is, indeed, an intimidating task to turn a group of gentleman politicians into an effective law making body. The new Parliament's members are easily offended by something: anticlerical demagoguery, bad grammar, offensive Catalan, Andalusian and Madrid accents, all the jealous, meanness and irrational passion of the over privileged or undereducated. Several have already resigned, saying that they could not abide such behavior. My mother would have called that 'drowning in a teacup'.

Begonia said in a pleading voice, "I say again that exhibiting portraits of peasants will be inflammatory. There is nothing redeeming about replacing religious and royal images in peasants' cottages with pictures of themselves. It is a subversion of our traditional ways."

She was about to continue when Luis Eduardo stood. "That is enough, Begonia! You are in my house, and I will hear no more criticisms of my wife. Her photographic project is noble and artistic, and that is all it is. Your unrestrained meanderings offend me and would hurt my father if he were here. I have decided to support the visit of *Misiones Pedagogicas* and Katherine's photographs will be exhibited. Now let us stop this hard talk and go to bed."

He raised Katherine from her seat, put her arm into his, and went into the house. Begonia stood up, paced back and forth, wringing her hands, and muttering to herself. I went to my rooms and Manuel strode off to his cottage.

A shudder went through me as I realized for the first time that the visit of *Misiones Pedagogicas* could have unpredictable consequences. It was not hard to imagine some sort of violence by either the conservatives or anarchists and then violence in response.

It had come as a shock for me to find out that an obscure political ideology like Anarchism was, sub rosa, flourishing in rural Spain. When Beltran told me that emerging political and social changes in Spain could ignite long standing anger and frustration, I didn't know what he meant. But I began to understand how actions could be unleashed that no one could predict or control. Even a modest educational program like *Misiones Pedagogicas* could turn dangerous without warning. Beltran and his class were determined to find a way out of the life they were forced to live, watching children starve when there was no work and die from lack of milk.

How could violence not be an inevitable part of that struggle? I did not sleep well that night.

CHAPTER EIGHT

Edwin's Spanish Connections

W hen Luis Eduardo's mother founded her school at Los Olivares, she hired a local person to teach essential reading, writing, and simple sums. Weekly religious instruction from the local priest prepared students for confession and their First Holy Communion. After she died, her husband, Don Carlo, kept the school open with the same teacher. When Katherine took over the school, she kept it operating, but wanted to improve its educational quality. So she hired Manuel in September, and brought me from England in June.

Spain's peasant tradition had always been that the entire family, including infants carried on the backs of their mothers, worked in the fields during harvests between September and December. Luis Eduardo decided to break that tradition by keeping the school open all year long. "A few children not working will not affect the productivity of the estate," he said, "and their education is a sound contribution to the students and their families."

From the beginning, I joined Manuel in the morning sessions at the school house, and was impressed with the way he organized the lessons. There were songs in Spanish to teach vocabulary, and lessons in writing out and memorizing the words in the songs. Addition and subtraction were taught using small painted boxes that had been constructed by the students' fathers, using wood and paint provided by the school. There was a map of Spain, another of the world for geography lessons, and a supply of big sheets of white paper, watercolor paints, brushes, and colored pencils for art lessons.

Each day there was a "word-of-the-day" written in big letters and put on the wall next to its definition. Lunch was brought from the main house in early afternoon. The students used cloth napkins with their initials embroidered by their mothers and kept them in napkin rings made from bits of rope. Friday was a cleanup day, the napkins were washed, the floor swept, and blackboards cleaned with water and then "polished" when they were dry to remove any streaks.

During their work, the students sang their songs over and over. After lunch, the students packed up their notebooks and utensils and stood in line to shake hands with Manuel, whom they called Sr. Professor Montilla. Afternoons, I tutored my boys in French, English, Geography, and Math at the main house. Beltran taught them to ride ponies three afternoons a week. Their younger sister Ottilie was still under the tutelage of her nanny, Mrs. Coleman, who followed old-fashioned nursery rules like making her lie down every day on a stiff board to give her good posture.

The families of the students made clear to their children that they must be serious about school. They washed every morning, combed their hair, and were never late. They sat quietly at their desks, stood when the teacher entered the classroom, and did not speak unless called upon. The students were not used to rules like this but tried hard to follow them. Manuel understood that and also knew that when corrections were necessary, he needed to be gentle about it.

Manuel added a rule of his own, banning the word "stupid." He said that this word was rude and hurtful and represented ignorance. There was no occasion when it would be allowed in the classroom or anywhere near the schoolhouse. Manuel was a genius at establishing trust with the students, and he made clear by his manner that he took them seriously. They responded by working hard.

Manuel was a remarkable teacher for his "young scholars," as he called them. He wore a shirt, tie and jacket every day, even when it was very hot, as a way of honoring the students. "This is what we wore at university," he told them, "and there is every reason to dress the same here as I did." The students came to admire him, and the school was calm and quiet.

I was in the classroom every morning with my two boys, and although they were treated like the other students, it was evident that they were very different. There was initially a sense of deference on the part of the village children toward Oscar and Leander, which Manuel and I addressed by saying firmly that in this classroom there would be no distinctions, that students were all equal, and were to treat each other as such. The students were skeptical about that. Nothing in their experience suggested that people would ever be treated the same, but seeing that such a thing was possible was one of many non-academic lessons they learned.

Oscar and Leander wore simple country clothes, but the other students wore little better than clean rags. This gave me the idea of giving all the students the same clothing, a kind of uniform that would enhance their sense of being part of a select group. Katherine was enthusiastic about this idea. She bought fabrics for the families to sew into trousers and shirts for the boys and dresses for the girls who got brightly colored ribbons. The villagers wrote a letter thanking Katherine and Luis Eduardo for this act of kindness. The students were no less impressed and wrote their own letter, pledging to be good students. Katherine framed both letters, which were hung on the wall of the schoolhouse.

One morning a boy hurt himself while cutting wood for the stove. He came into the schoolhouse bleeding profusely, causing an uproar among the students. Manuel ordered the students to sit quietly at their desks, as he tore down curtains to make a tourniquet. I quickly took Oscar and Leander to the main house. Begonia indicated that the wounded boy would not be allowed inside the main house, but that I was to take him to his family's house in the village.

Beltran was nowhere to be found, so I decided to use the family carriage instead of a farm wagon, as a way to make the boy comfortable, planning to carefully cover the leather seats with horse blankets. As a stable boy hooked up a horse to the carriage, I ordered a farm hand to drive it and another one to ride a horse alongside. We stopped at the schoolhouse to pick up the wounded boy, where Manuel helped me to load him into the carriage. I then drove to the village, where I found his family's house. Manuel had reconvened the class in order to quiet the students. I could hear their songs as we left for the village. I thought admiringly how British was Manuel's reaction, to carry on so calmly.

I drove the carriage slowly to the village to keep the boy comfortable. His shirt was stained with blood, and he was drowsy. His mother and two sisters became agitated when they saw the blood, wringing their hands and keening. Neighbor women came to help. The boy's older brother arrived a few minutes later, obviously upset but calm in a dignified and manly way. He re-bandaged the wound and the boy then fell into a deep sleep.

The boy's older brother introduced himself to me as Guillermo Perez and said his wounded little brother was called Alberto. As we shook hands, Guillermo fervently expressed gratitude that his brother had been brought in a family carriage instead of a farm wagon and by the young foreign gentleman himself. Beltran arrived and after examining Alberto's wound told the family it would heal in a few days, with an admonition to let him know if there were complications. His presence was calming, and the atmosphere in the room became less tense. Alberto's mother kissed Beltran's hand, with tears in her eyes. Beltran said nothing but embraced her, murmuring a few words of comfort. He told the stable boys to leave a horse for me and to return to Los Olivares with the wagon.

Beltran and I bid farewell to the family and walked our horses to the main plaza. As we approached the tavern, Beltran asked me to stay outside as he went in. As I waited, women and children gathered, staring quietly. I was trying to bide my time and not look foolish as I stood there, so I asked one of the boys what his name was. The boy's eyes widened, he stood straight and said proudly, "I am called Octavio Alcazar Vaquero Ladron de Guevara."

I shook the boy's hand and said, "Oh, what a grand name! I have only three--Edwin, Benedict, and Fitzgerald. I come from a faraway land called England."

The boy looked puzzled and said, "Another land? But all the world is Spain, so what is 'England'"?

I realized the boy was too young to have attended school, so had never heard that there were other countries in the world beside Spain. I said that it took four days to travel to get to England, which was an island where English was spoken, not Spanish.

The group looked amazed at this news, so I spoke a few words in English and Spanish. "You say *cielo* and I say sky. You say *pan tostado* and I say toasted bread. I say olives, you say *aceitunas*." Everyone giggled and smiled, as my English words must have sounded to them like a baby's babbling.

Beltran came out of the tavern in time to observe my interaction with the boy and motioned that we were leaving. When the two of us were out of sight of the village, Beltran turned off the road, dismounting in woods near a stream. It was cool and shady so we walked a few minutes until Beltran abruptly said: "I am going to talk to you now about things that might be dangerous for you to know, and about which you must tell no one."

I faced Beltran directly. "It is an honor for me to be taken into your confidence. What you tell me will remain secret."

Beltran shook my hand. "That is just what I had hoped for." As we walked along the stream, Beltran continued. "Many years ago, I was the leader of the Anarchists in this district. People remember me in that role and expect me to listen to them and to guide them. I stopped because I was getting old and wanted more time to myself and to be with my wife.

I also stopped because I came to see that Anarchism's goal to establish a free and fair society can never succeed if it is built on the destruction of existing society. So I quit the Anarchists and have not been involved since, although people know me in that role."

"There is something else. I once had a son named Ignacio, the pride of my life. He was very smart and taught himself to read far beyond what he was taught at Dona Luisa's school. But he was hot-headed and went to work at a nearby farm. He was killed when a dead tree limb fell on him. Since then, Consolata's and my life has been melancholy. But it has made me happy to help you become a Spanish gentleman and, I hope, a friend."

"In the tavern is an old comrade of mine who wants me to become active again in politics, which would mean getting involved in violent activity. I refused because once violence starts, it spreads like fire through dry corn. I am telling you this because I want you to be alert to suspicious activity. I do not think there is any danger to us at Los Olivares, but you are a foreigner, something unusual and confusing for people here. Anarchists may associate you with foreign ownership of industry and railroads, something they believe exploits Spanish workers and so must be destroyed and then rebuilt under Spanish ownership. Be watchful and if you see anything out of the ordinary, tell me about it."

"You must always be aware that you can never be one of us, and what you think of as a simple social interaction can come back to haunt you. That little interaction with the boy in the crowd outside the tavern, for example, is ordinary for you but for that boy, it will be one of the highlights of his life - talking to a foreign gentleman in front of his friends and holding his own. Singling him out that way could lead to jealousy and torment by his cronies."

Beltran stopped talking and sat down next to me. His manner made me suspect that he was holding something back, and I asked him if he was.

"You are right, Edwin, I am not telling you what is really on my mind. Perhaps I suspect that, like my Ignacio, you want to become involved in the changes that are coming. Am I correct? As you are becoming aware, Spain is a place where the suffering of people from indolent and selfish leaders is everywhere apparent. That has never changed. What do you think that you, as an outsider, could possibly do about these evil things?"

I thought for a while. "I am not sure how to answer you, Beltran," I admitted, finally "I know very little about Spanish politics and have no idea how I could participate. But I feel compelled to understand more of what is happening in Spain. I imagine that one thing I could do is perhaps get to know people like Alberto's older brother, Guillermo. He seemed about my age, and perhaps there is a way for us to get to know each other, and in the process, learn things from each other."

Would it really possible, I wondered, that Guillermo and I could bridge over the things that separated us? Guillermo seemed intelligent and perhaps he was curious about the larger world that I represented. I was equally curious about his life. I decided to trust my instincts in these matters but was also dimly aware that my interest in getting to know Guillermo and other peasants could become a kind of condescension, which made me uncomfortable.

"Becoming friends with Guillermo is more complicated than you know," Beltran said,. "You would be stepping over formidable lines that separate class in Spain. But since you were so kind to his brother, a return visit to check on the boy would be appropriate. The family would insist that you stay for a glass of wine and of course, you must accept. Perhaps you and Guillermo could walk to the tavern for a hand of cards, or go fishing together on a Sunday afternoon. Guillermo would certainly not own a horse, so you should walk to the village as a gesture, that will certainly be noticed, for which Guillermo will be grateful. It will be a compliment to you if Guillermo asks you to sit with his family as they watch a Sunday *paseo*."

Beltran suggested that I wait for a week or so before visiting the wounded boy, Alberto, and his family. "During that time you and I will stop at the tavern to let people know that we are friends. I rarely visit the village nowadays and being seen together will send the right signal about your subsequent visit."

"What is that signal, Beltran?"

"As you seem to be learning, Spanish society is based on long-accepted social classifications. You are in a world with customs that you know little about. I'm not sure why you have done such a thing, but you must be aware that as a young educated foreigner you should do nothing that might be seen as cause for suspicion. The villagers have never seen someone like you and will gossip about it. For that reason, take care how you carry yourself, how you interact with people. I knew Guillermo's grandfather when I was involved in village life, and suspect that you and his grandson will get along well."

"Send a note to him that you would like to visit next Sunday afternoon, when he and everyone else in the village will not be working. The boy's mother will appreciate that because it will give her time to arrange to have wine and, if necessary, to borrow dishes from a neighbor. Your visit will enhance the status of the family, and the village will be impressed that you are making a social call of this kind, that you have good manners, and there is nothing to worry about. Consolata will make little cakes and put them into a box to take with you and tie it with silk ribbons, which will be kept and worn by one of Guillermo's sisters on holidays."

I asked Beltran if I could give Alberto a knife that has my initials on it. Beltran at first said no; he thought it too generous a gift for a poor peasant. I said that it was a gift from my uncle. For many years I used it, but I no longer did and wanted to give it to someone who would like to have it. Beltran said that telling that story would make the gift acceptable because it was meant to be a tool rather than just a decoration and a knife was high on the list of useful objects. He then said that if I told a bit of its history the knife could be an appropriate gift.

"As you are coming to understand, our social rules are precise and missteps are remembered forever. At the Feria at Seville a year from now, you and Manuel will ride next to Luis Eduardo alongside the old yellow-painted Landau carriage that will be carrying Dona Begonia, Dona Katherine, and her children. By that time, you must ride well enough to be noticed as the young foreigner who knows the Spanish rulebook. These judgments of form are both serious and nonsensical, but they are part of life here, and it is invigorating to do them well." I was grateful for Beltran's advice, and for his concern that I not inadvertently make social blunders.

We mounted our horses and rode in silence to Los Olivares. When we dismounted, I made a point of holding his hand for a few moments after shaking it. We smiled at each other. I said, "Thank you."

On a Thursday afternoon I sent a stable boy with a note to Guillermo, and on Sunday at three o'clock I set off on foot. As I walked the half hour it took to get to the village, I thought about how interesting it was to be among people so different from myself, yet feel so much a part of their life. I grew up surrounded by social edicts, but Spanish manners seemed to be both more elaborate and more defining of status than what I had encountered at home. I was grateful for Beltran's guidance.

When I arrived at Guillermo's cottage he was sitting on a chair out front. He stood up, inclined his head in greeting, and shook hands. He was tall and muscular, with black hair, dark eyes, and deeply tanned face and hands. His fingernails were clean and his black hair was glistening from pomade, which all Spanish men used. He was wearing a white shirt open at the neck and a wide brimmed black hat. I presented him the box with the red ribbon and said, "This is for your mother," and we went inside the house. Guillermo introduced me to his mother, his two sisters and a very old man that he said was his uncle.

This visit was the first time I had an opportunity to have a good look at the inside of a peasant house. The entrance opened into a little corridor with three doors. One led to the kitchen, the second to the bedroom, and the third to the rear of the house. The corridor seemed to be the coolest place in the house and was furnished with a wooden chest, a couple of benches, with an old rug on a floor of hard earth. We went into the kitchen and sat on an old straight-backed sofa that Guillermo's mother said grandly was the pride of the family. There was a table with a tablecloth, several chairs, and wildflowers in a glass jar. I was impressed by how clean and tidy the house was.

I went to the boy, Alberto, and shook his hand. After a few moments of awkward silence, I took out the sliver pocketknife and showed it to him. "As you can see this knife is engraved with my initials. I no longer use it, but it is still very sharp, so I want you to be careful when you open it. My uncle gave it to me when I was about your age, and it is an honor for me to give it to you as a token of friendship."

Alberto's eyes widened, and he hesitated before taking the knife, looking at Guillermo for a signal that accepting it was allowed. Guillermo smiled and nodded, after which Alberto took the knife and carefully turned it over in his hand. He looked at me gravely. "Senor, thank you for this gift. I have never had a knife, but now I have the best knife in the world."

His brother clapped him on the shoulder and smiled. "Alberto is a lucky boy to get such a great gift. Many thanks, sir, for your kindness to him when he was hurt and now for your generosity to him by giving him something that he never thought he would be able to have."

The box with red ribbons was a great success. Guillermo's mother opened it carefully and put the cakes on a plate. The sisters admired the ribbon, the younger one tying it around her hair while her sister poured wine into little glasses. The cakes were then handed around by the mother. She thanked me for coming and for bringing what she called "these lovely sweets which we have never had." When I said that Beltran's wife had prepared them, the old lady smiled and asked me to thank her too. We all sat and began to talk at the same time in the way Spaniards do.

Guillermo suggested that we go for a walk. After I said goodbye to the family, we left the house and walked toward the main square. This little promenade seemed important as an indication that we were friends. As we chatted, I leaned into him arm in arm.

Two story houses faced the plaza. Women strolled arm-in-arm in the strange solitude of Spaniards, or in loud interminable conversations, with everyone talking at the same time. The older women dressed in black and the men and children in slightly less somber colors, all the clothes in tatters. Everyone old wore hats. Many of the older people supported themselves using polished sticks as canes or leaned into younger people for support. Some people, crippled by age and infirmities, were tended by companions as they made their way.

We went into the small tavern. Conversations stopped as we entered, and everyone stared. Guillermo shook hands with the men and introduced me to them. They were drinking anise or wine and eating black olives from little plates. Guillermo ordered anise for both of us, for which he was careful to pay.

The door to the plaza was open, letting in sunlight, revealing that the place was gloomy and disheveled, littered with the little pieces of paper which passed for napkins and which were discarded on the floor, a tradition in Spanish bars. At first, no one spoke to us while the two of us stood at the bar chatting. Soon an old man approached us and said in broken English, "Are you from London? I was there once when I was a sailor in the Spanish Navy, many years ago. My name is Leonardo Cabrera." He smiled at me as we shook hands, enjoying his status as someone who spoke English.

I said that I was from Dublin, Ireland, actually, but I was at school in England and often went to London. "When were you there?"

"Sixty years ago, when I was about your age, I suppose. London was an immense place for a simple farmer-sailor like me, but was a great thing to see, and I have always remembered it."

"And he never ceases to remind all of us about the place as though he was there last week," someone said loudly, clapping the old man's shoulder and grinning along with him and the rest of the men.

111

Guillermo addressed the room. "This young Englishman has come to live among us, and was very kind to my brother when he hurt himself at the schoolhouse last week. He brought Alberto home in a family carriage, mind you, in order to make him comfortable. I am forever grateful for that, and thank him for coming to my house today to visit us."

At that Guillermo and the men in the tavern raised their glasses in a silent toast. I responded by saying, "Thank you for your hospitality today," and then in English, "and thank you, Senor Cabrera, for telling me about your visit to London and for your excellent English." At that another silent toast was made, and people went back to their separate conversations, and we left.

Guillermo took me by the arm. "Let me show you the best thing in our village." We stopped at a fountain pouring water into a circular basin sheltered by the branches of four trees placed symmetrically around it, called *La Verdura*. "Water runs continuously even in the hot summer, a never-ending source of clear fresh water, great comfort during the hot summer. The fountain was built by Don Carlo, and is the pride of the village."

Stopping for a moment at the edge of a rectangular pool, he pointed out a long slab of stone where women knelt to wash clothes, surrounded by stone columns that formerly supported a roof over the washing area.

We walked back to Guillermo's cottage, said our farewells with declarations to get together again, and I walked back to Los Olivares.

Beltran had been right about not arriving on horseback, thereby presenting myself as a humble person who knew how to pay his respects to the family and especially to Guillermo. The visit was a success and paved the way for me to see another part of Spanish life.

Beltran was glad that the visit had gone well and encouraged my friendship with Guillermo. But he was also cautious about this friendship. I was too, I suppose, but I wanted the friendship to be straightforward and honest, in the Spanish way. Beltran thought that Luis Eduardo should be consulted about my interest in friendship with Guillermo.

Luis Eduardo said, "I am intrigued. Why do you want to be friends? What will either of you get from it?"

I thought for a few moments and said, "Well, that is certainly not clear to me. But friendship could be an opportunity for me to talk with Guillermo about *Misiones Pedagogicas.*"

"And what makes you think that peasants need motivation to participate in *Misiones Pedagogicas*?" Luis Eduardo asked.

"The seriousness with which the families and their students attend the school tells us the answer," I replied. "They greatly value education and are protective of it when it is available to them. They cannot imagine a group like *Misiones Pedagogicas* visiting their village, so talking with them about it will help them understand what will be happening."

Luis Eduardo said that Begonia would be astonished and then infuriated at the idea of "one of us" becoming a personal friend of a peasant. "This would be a blow to Begonia's hope that you would become a Spanish gentleman. For her, the idea of even stepping foot in our fields or olive groves is totally beyond her imagination."

The friendship among Guillermo, Beltran and me was oddly easy-going, as though we had known each other a long time. We all felt this and spent more and more time together on weekends.

I asked Beltran to teach Guillermo to ride a horse. He graciously extended himself to do so. We three roamed the countryside far and wide, talking continuously. Guillermo regaled us with horror stories about the treatment of workers. Manuel got worked up about the endless oppression from big landowners and how he earnestly hoped for change. I told them about the places I'd seen: Paris, Venice, Istanbul, Vienna. We very much enjoyed each other's company and were full of high spirits. How glad I was that we could be together, and how exhilarating to become friends with people so different from me.

I decided to ask Luis Eduardo and Beltran if they would allow the three of us to take the train to Madrid and stay there for a few days. They quickly agreed, and Luis Eduardo arranged for us to stay with Don Carlos. Begonia was furious at the prospect of a peasant from Los Olivares staying at her apartment but was overruled by her husband. Eduardo bought them train tickets and gave us pocket money. Beltran took us to Granada, where we got on the train to Madrid.

From the train station, we walked to Don Carlos' apartment where he received us, took us to our rooms, and gave us lunch. Guillermo was thrilled as we went for a long walk through the city, and then to a cafe for dinner. The next day we went to the Naval Museum, the Museum of Royal Carriages, and Retiro Park where we had lunch at an outdoor cafe. We took trams, a ride on the Metro Line #1 that had just opened, and visited the great water reservoir which was the pride of the city, bringing fresh water from nearby mountains. We looked at the Royal Palace and the Opera House, the Plaza Major, and went into the National Library, then the most extensive library in the world. There was a vast reading room designed to hold three hundred readers surrounded by three floors of open bookshelves. The library's collection consisted of more than sixteen million items, including books, maps, and newspapers, and other printed materials.

Guillermo was speechless. "For me," he said finally, "I never imagined that such a thing existed, a palace of books. And that the general public can go in when they want to! Not to be able to read is yet another thing that keeps us enslaved to our miserable lives! One day I will learn to read, and when I do, it will be because of this visit." Then he bowed his head as if before a grand personage and stood in front of the building for a few minutes with tears in his eyes.

Guillermo's gesture moved us immensely, and we put our arms around Guillermo's shoulders in silent homage to our friend, this remarkable man.

The other thing we loved was watching Madrid police insist that everyone cross the road only at the lights, and only when the lights were green. Madrilènos stood on opposite curbs, impatient to spring at each other when the whistle went off. Then they played with the traffic like matadors with bulls, seeing how near they could get without accident, and irritating the drivers into pressing the bellows on their horns and releasing a raucous noise. If pedestrians did not submit to the tyranny of stoplights, they got a fine of two pesetas. We noticed that the game was to hang about until the policeman was engaged writing in his book the receipt for one of these fines, and then with smiles fit for the heavens, to dash across against the red lights and escape in triumph. What adventure they made of crossing a street!

I was impressed by Guillermo's insatiable curiosity. When we visited one of the great bookstores on Gran Via, Guillermo was astonished by the thousands of books, dozens of Spanish and foreign newspapers, as well as colored prints of famous paintings and snowy mountain vistas, one of which he purchased. Guillermo also bought a gold pin for his wife and souvenirs for his children. We were very happy to be together on this adventure and increasingly aware of the deepening friendship among the three of us.

On the train back to Granada Guillermo was uncharacteristically quiet. Finally, he said, "It is as though I am awakening from a dream, seeing things that I could never have imagined. The royal carriages were especially amazing because I can hardly believe that they are used to carry people on ordinary streets."

I replied, "I am glad that we have been together in Madrid. It is a place that few of your compatriots will ever see the way you have: staying in a luxurious apartment, having pocket money to visit places and buy treats like *churros de chocolate,* spending time walking through the city, stopping for coffee or a beer. I suppose one could say that for these few days we left your world and you visited mine."

Guillermo stared at us. 'Guillermo stared at us. "I will never forget our time in Madrid and will be forever grateful to have been there together. We all know that I will never visit Madrid again, that there is no place for me in Madrid. I saw how the servant looked at me when he opened the apartment door. He saw the two of you and smiled, but he looked at my hands and saw a peasant in fine clothes, and he frowned. His opinions about us were fully formed before we arrived. I am someone he scorns, even fears. Madrid must be full of people like that."

Guillermo grabbed our hands. "You are not like that, either or you. Your kindness to me and our friendship is the highpoint of my life. I will never forget you, but after you leave, there will be no reason for you to remember me. By the time I am forty years old you will be entering the prime of your life, but I will be old and infirm, if not dead. Your children will be well fed and will go to school, while mine will be ill, weak and starving, and will learn nothing more than how to read a little and do sums. Our fates were cast long ago."

I was impressed by Guillermo's courage and honesty about his future. But I was not so sure that it was as inevitable as he assumed.

Manuel was moved by Guillermo's speech, too. "Guillermo, we are well into the twentieth century and are now in the midst of immense social and political tumult," he told him. "Spain has just elected a progressive government, making radical change possible. I hope that participation in *Misiones Pedagogicas* will be the village's first opportunity to be introduced to the larger world." The three of us lapsed into the doldrums of the long train ride to Granada, where Beltran met us at the station. I felt that I was coming home.

CHAPTER NINE

School House Vandalism

S
ometime before the arrival of the *Misiones Pedagogicas*, Katherine
and Consolata began taking the photographs to the family's old
house in the village, where they would be exhibited. There were
pictures of everyone in the household at Los Olivares except Begonia,
who would not participate, and photos of farm workers and their families, all in simple black frames behind glass.

I endeared myself to Guillermo and the peasants by working with
them, mowing hay under the blazing Spanish sun. They were surprised
by my stamina, and everyone liked that I had mastered the Spanish
way of telling dry, self-deprecating jokes, not a small achievement for
a foreigner.

Local officials, landowners and members of old families were invited
to see Katherine's photos before *Misiones Pedagogicas* arrived and before
the exhibition was officially opened. They were shocked to see portraits

of peasants presented in the same format as the owners of Los Olivares, dumbfounded that a foreigner married to "one of us" would, under the guise of an artistic project, challenge the long-standing assumption that peasants are nothing more than a fearful mob.

During breaks in the mowing I talked with the workers about the events to be taking place during the visit of *Misiones Pedagogicas*, and encouraged them to participate. Luis Eduardo announced the suspension of fieldwork during the weeklong visit, and added that the school would be closed. There was happy anticipation about the free dinners every night in the main plaza.

One afternoon in the fields the workers and I saw a cloud of dust gathering on the main road from the village. I knew it was the arrival of the trucks and cars bringing the artifacts to be part of *Misiones Pedagogicas* activities. We put aside our implements and rushed to the caravan. A huge vehicle covered in canvas led the way. When it got to the village, it stopped at the Town Hall and began unloading large rectangular objects called "paintings," a word the peasants had never heard. The guests were led to the house where they would be staying, took their suitcases inside, and clambered up the stairs to their rooms with the help of village women and children.

People came to stare at the spectacle of *Misiones Pedagogicas* arriving and unpacking all sorts of unknown objects. There were components for building a temporary stage, a wind-up Victrola, boxes of books, wood to make shelves for a library, and a gasoline generator. Meanwhile, great rectangular objects were taken into City Hall and removed from their canvas coverings. The village people were astonished to see life-size pictures of noblemen and women on horseback dressed in elaborate clothes.

At dusk, the unloading stopped. Fires were lit for cooking paella, wine casks were opened, and the bread that had been baked by Consolata that day was put on the tables, next to heaps of tomatoes and salad greens. Local people brought eating utensils and chairs for themselves and their guests. Everyone greeted each other as music on guitar, drums and trumpets began, and many people danced. Finally, after midnight, people returned home, and the guests to their lodgings, everyone full of good cheer.

The next morning Manuel was awakened by commotion at the schoolhouse and rushed there to investigate. When the vandals saw him, they fled, shouting curses.

On the front of the little building was hastily painted,

MUERTE A LA AUSENCIA DE DIOS EN ESTA ESCUELA
(Death to the absence of God in this school) and *VIVA ESPANA!*

Manuel was horrified at the damage. Windows had been broken, the carefully tended vegetable garden was destroyed, and dead plants scattered all over the place. Inside the schoolhouse, a place which had always been kept so neat and tidy, books were thrown onto the floor and destroyed by having their pages ripped out, desks were overturned and damaged, blackboards were shattered, and ink had been poured on the wood floor and spattered on walls.

The peasants were arriving at the schoolhouse and immediately began cleaning up the mess left by the vandals, slowly becoming angry as they discovered the extent of the damage. The vandalism violated their bedrock belief that education was the only way for their children to escape their humiliating lives.

In a spontaneous outpouring of rage the men marched to the main plaza, and gathered in front of the barracks of the Guardia Civil. The crowd shouted and threw stones, breaking windows. The Guardia ordered them to disband, only to be met with raucous jeers, insults, and increased volleys of stone throwing. The villagers would not leave. Staying in the plaza was a kind of victory for the village, generating shouting and cheerful backslapping.

After a short time, the Guardia Civil began firing through the broken windows, scattering most of the crowd into the safety of the streets leading away from the plaza. Rubbish was piled against the main door of the church. Guillermo and I and a few others crouched behind the long, black benches at the middle of the plaza, uneasily watching an unsuccessful attempt to set the church on fire.

I begged Guillermo to leave, but he made it clear that he was determined to revenge the new vandalism of the schoolhouse. "Edwin, you know by now that we have nothing but the education given to us at Los Olivares. I have learned from you that I am not nothing. I am a man and must make choices in my life. Now is the time for me to confront one of the evils in our lives."

I felt that Guillermo was right. I told him we were in this together and I stayed with him.

It had become terribly hot. Women and girls brought strips of cloth to bind the wounds of demonstrators. Everyone was very agitated. People rushed around the plaza looking for friends and family, calling out their names. Then, an eerie silence filled the plaza.

Guillermo and I, along with a few others, had taken shelter behind the plaza's long black benches. Every few minutes we stood up waving our arms and shouting insults at the Civil Guard, which provoked a barrage of gunfire from them. I remember a sudden jolt like lightening, burning like fire. Guillermo dragged me from the plaza, leaving a long trail of blood. I was conscious enough to feel intense pain in my stomach. I vaguely remember that Guillermo covered me with his jacket and talked to me as he held me close. I pleaded for water.

Guillermo later told me that Beltran found us and shouted for bandages and tourniquets. There was pandemonium as the shooting continued and people ran from the plaza, shouting curses as they fled.

Beltran left the Plaza and galloped to Los Olivares. He found Luis Eduardo, told him what was happening and that I had been shot. Beltran rushed to the stables to get a farm wagon laid with straw to pick up Guillermo and me. Luis Eduardo left immediately for Granada in his Ford car to get his family doctor.

Beltran drove the farm wagon helter-skelter to the plaza, stopping to collect Manuel at his cottage on the way. I was put into the wagon with him and Guillermo, who I was dimly aware was comforting me. We left at full speed until Guillermo shouted that I was moaning and shaking uncontrollably, and began to succumb. Beltran slowed the wagon and gave the reins to the stable boy as he climbed in the back. I drifted in and out of consciousness, unable to speak, as he repeated over and over, "Edwin, my boy, I am here with you. We all are here. Do not leave us."

At Los Olivares, I was carried to a cot brought from the house so I could be taken into Luis Eduardo's study on the first floor. Consolata and Katherine changed the bandages and put cold compresses on my feverish forehead. I was in pain but conscious. Consolata and Katherine were trying to cool me by vigorously moving their fans around my head. They later told me that eventually I fell into a coma, until Luis Eduardo arrived in the late afternoon with his doctor. His examination revealed that a bullet had entered my stomach. I had a high fever, and a lot of blood had been lost. The bullet needed to be removed surgically at a hospital, the nearest of which was in Granada, a four-hour drive over bad roads. The doctor warned that such a journey would be fatal, as it would likely cause internal bleeding.

The doctor injected morphine and the pain subsided. I felt myself drifting to sleep. Manuel stayed with Guillermo and me for the rest of the day and through the night. The doctor stayed overnight. In the morning, the prognosis was grim, as it was unclear whether there was damage to a major organ or artery.

A telegram was sent to my father, warning that I had been shot and that he should come as soon as he could. I was glad of that but there had never been a crisis of this sort in my family and I was apprehensive about how Papa would react. He sent a return telegram saying that he was leaving Dublin and would be at Granada in four days. The prospect of meeting my father under these circumstances filled me with dread. He had been opposed to my coming to Spain instead of returning to Dublin to join the family business. I only wrote to him occasionally, so he knew little about my life there. He would, of course, be horrified that I had been shot, and more so when he discovered that it had happened during a political manifestation.

Luis Eduardo informed the doctor that a nearby village was on the rail line for the Madrid-Granada train and it could be arranged by telephone for a train to make an emergency stop there. In the first class cars, there was a private compartment with a single bed, a chair, and a sink that was usually available and could be reserved. The doctor agreed that taking the train to Granada would minimize discomfort and was worth the risk. He would stay on the train with his patient. Luis Eduardo succeeded in getting the train to make an emergency stop the next morning to pick me up.

The next day Beltran, Guillermo, and Manuel prepared the farm-wagon to take me to the train. My bed was lifted into the wagon, and Beltran drove with the doctor sitting next to him, and Guillermo and Manuel in the back with me. I was put into the bed in the private compartment with the doctor sitting nearby. Katherine and Luis Eduardo went by car to the hospital in Granada to arrange for an ambulance to meet the train and rush me immediately to the hospital, where surgeons would be waiting to receive me. I slept at the hospital through a morphine haze with the vague awareness that Beltran stayed in my room all night. The others slept at a house of Luis Eduardo's relatives.

After the operation to remove the bullet from my abdomen, the doctor and the surgeon declared the surgery a success, and said I could return to Los Olivares by train in a few days, after which recuperation would take weeks.

Everyone returned to Los Olivares excerpt Beltran, who stayed in my room day and night until I was ready to go back, sitting quietly at my bedside most of the time. We did not talk much, but I was enormously comforted that he was there with me. Although I was in pain, I felt completely safe. His being there kept me from feeling alone in this strange and foreign place.

When we left the hospital, an ambulance took Beltran and me to the train where I was installed in a first-class seat that had been reconfigured so that the back was nearly flat. Katherine and Luis Eduardo were waiting when the train arrived, the car filled with pillows and blankets. I was awake during the drive to Los Olivares where Consolata met us at the house along with Guillermo, Manuel, and household staff. I was taken into Luis Eduardo's study, which had been reconfigured as a kind of hospital room with a proper bed. Guillermo and Manuel stayed for the rest of the day. All of this reminded me that I had become part of the emotional life of Los Olivares and especially deepened my gratitude that the three of us had become true friends.

A few days later Begonia came to see me, took my hands in hers, kissed me gently and said, "I have learned things from you, young man, which had never occurred to me. I don't like some of them, but I am grateful for your having been here with us. I hope you understand that my set-to with Katherine about my spilled wine was merely my feeble attempt to help her understand our ways. You took it the wrong way, I fear. I ask your forgiveness for my having expressed myself badly."

She stiffened slightly as I managed to say, " Thank you for coming to see me, but it is not to me to whom you should apologize, but to Katherine and Luis Eduardo."

Begonia appeared nonplussed by my impertinence, but said nothing and immediately left the room.

I then heard her proclaiming loudly to Katherine that she was horrified by the gossip that would inevitably begin circulating in Madrid about my having been shot. She said that she was feeling disfranchised by her family's attitude toward her complaints, on the other hand. "This unsavory business," she exclaimed, "is going to ruin my reputation."

Katherine became exasperated and retorted, "Be still, Begonia, or go to Madrid and leave the rest of us to help our patient recover."

Begonia declared that since her help was not wanted, she would leave at once. She flounced out, calling for her maid and her driver, and was soon gone in a cloud of dust. I felt relieved that she had left.

Two days later my father arrived at Granada by train where he was met by Luis Eduardo and Katherine. He is a small man, precise in manner, neatly dressed, with piercing gray eyes behind wire-rimmed glasses, giving the impression of calm, decency, and lack of pretension. His emotions, from lack of exercise, had disappeared almost altogether. Adaptability and curiosity, he had found, did just as well.

After a light supper, he went to bed and slept well. The next morning he was up early, took a stroll around the place before joining Katherine and Eduardo on the loggia for a breakfast.

Luis Eduardo suggested that my father might want to talk with Manuel and Guillermo. "The three of them spend a lot of time together, and they can tell you about Edwin's life here."

The rest of the day my father spent by himself, walking through the olive orchards, resting in the garden, and visiting my two friends. Late into the evening, he sat by my bed and began to relay the story of their conversation.

After dinner, he had walked to Manuel's cottage. The door was ajar, so he knocked and went in just as Guillermo arrived. Manuel welcomed them.

He started the conversation by thanking the two of them for meeting with him, and told them that I had always been a good son, quiet and thoughtful, although by the time I graduated from Cambridge he was aware of my restlessness and wanting to go somewhere "exotic," to stretch out, to meet new people on my terms.

Manuel had spoken up first, saying that it was a kind of miracle that this generous, lively young man could come from nowhere and that my father's description of me before coming there was not the way he thought of me. He said I was a wonderful friend to Guillermo and him, full of high spirits.

My father especially wanted to hear about the circumstances under which I was shot, which Luis Eduardo had told him was during a political incident. He told me forcefully that my becoming involved in that sort of thing was hard for him to understand.

Guillermo apparently was anxious to talk and after asking Manuel to translate his comments, as he spoke no English, and told my father that he knew how I was shot because he was there with me when it happened. He said that one night our schoolhouse was badly vandalized, and as it was the only one in the district, it was much beloved, so the vandalism enraged the villagers. They gathered in a raucous demonstration in front of the barracks of the Guardia Civil. The noise of the commotion reached Los Olivares, bringing us to the village to investigate. I joined the villagers as part of an angry crowd that attacked the barracks of the Guardia Civil. In retaliation, the demonstrators were fired upon, and I was, unfortunately, shot.

My father was dumbfounded that I had allowed myself to become involved in the politics of a foreign country and nearly die because of it. He was surprised at my recklessness and never would have thought that of me, and all of this was very difficult for him to understand.

Guillermo talked fast and excitedly about the friendship the three of us had, about our exhilarating trip together to Madrid, about my working in the fields. He told him my nickname was *'Nosotros Extranjero Amiable'*, which Manuel translated as "our friendly foreigner."

He also said earnestly that your being his friend had changed his life, that you took a special interest in him, helping him understand that the changes being talked about in Madrid could lead to a better future for his family and himself, an unimaginable idea when you were struggling to stay alive. He said he would always be grateful to me for that, because until then he had never heard anyone talk about the future, except itinerant anarchists, saying that justice could only come about after the destruction of Spain's unfair system.

We sat silently for a while until my I stood, thanked Manuel and Guillermo for talking so openly with me, I shook their hands earnestly, and came to see you.

My father knocked lightly on my door, opened it, came inside saying that he had just come from seeing Guillermo and Manuel. He sat on a chair that he pulled close to my bed and took my hand in his, and asked how I was feeling.

"Much better," I said, "although the morphine I take makes me groggy so I don't always think clearly. Please ask Consolata for tea, and it will make me more alert." He left for a few moments, came back, smiled, and said, "Tea is on its way."

Consolata came in, looked at me intensely, poured, and left.

We looked at each other solemnly until I finally said brightly, "Manuel and Guillermo are great friends. Knowing them has opened me to life in the village and the fields where I sometimes work with Guillermo and the peasants. Thank you for talking with them, Papa."

He replied, "Our chat was very interesting, and I can see what good friends the three of you must be." Then he crossed his arms and said abruptly, "I am sorry to say that I am irritated that you would get involved in Spanish life to the degree that you barely escaped death. That is so unlike you, Edwin, and so irresponsible, risking your life... for what? You can never be anything but an outsider in Spain. You're mistaking rash action for heroism. You are my only son, and life will never be the same if you leave us. Taking pride at having put your life at risk must be something you learned here. How did you become so thoughtless and self-centered that you were insensitive to the grief that would be caused by your death? I am confused and disappointed."

I listened quietly and replied, "Of course I know that my death would have affected a lot of people, and am full of regret to have put myself at such risk. But there is unimaginable injustice here, Papa, and I cannot just sit by. I would never have been allowed to interact with the sort of misery that exists here, which I now realize must have existed in Dublin when I was growing up, and most likely still does."

I was more than a little surprised at the audacious way I was speaking to my father, but I continued, looking directly at him. "I have thought a lot about our life in Dublin, at Cambridge and now in Spain, and if you don't mind, I would like to tell you some things that I am beginning to understand about myself."

It was clear that he was unsure what he should say or do. He sat up straight, unfolded his arms and said curtly, "Please do," his body language making clear that he was not looking forward to this little talk. But once I began, the words rolled off my tongue, seeming to emanate from a deeper part of myself.

I took a deep breath. "When I left London, nothing about my life was in doubt. I lived with long-standing certainties. For a long time I had thought of myself in both third person--'Who is Edwin?' and the first person--'Who am I?' This has always been the way for me to understand myself and my place in the world. Coming to Spain seemed to be just another step toward an interesting future, marching ahead like a well-trained hunting dog. I wanted to astonish everyone with my decision to go somewhere unexpected and also to be pleased with myself about that."

"I realized early on that the most significant things in my life were on the surface, the things that were easy to be judged: how one dressed, the correctness of table manners and social behavior, deference to parents, teachers, strangers. There was always a sense that violation of these norms would bring a kind of banishment.

"Aunt Lucrecia's imprecation that one must be trained to 'not make too much of things' defined correct behavior in Britain. The fact was, I never imagined that there could be an alternative. I never gave a second thought to the fact that our life was devoid of emotion or that there could be any reason to deviate from the strictures of existing form."

"I have thought a lot about the comfortable environment that you provided for our family. The sense of security that I grew up with was shattered when I spent time with the wounded soldiers, as they recovered at our horse farm. Until then, I had no interest in a life centered on riding and the culture it generates, something that I always knew disappointed you and my mother. But a life that was focused on horses, riding-to-hounds and attending Hunt Balls always seemed to me ostentatious and pointless."

"That is, until I had contact with those wounded soldiers and saw how being around horses was so healing for them. They groomed them, walked them, and, if they knew how to ride, were allowed to mount them and be led for walks. Sometimes I would read to them their letters from their families, listen to them tell stories about the war, and reminisce about their life before going off to war. Occasionally, they would cry when I was with them, telling me that I reminded them of their old selves, and how frightened they were about being invalids.

But they were so grateful to be in such a beautiful, quiet place after the terrible experiences they had endured. As you can imagine, I had no idea that our civilized world could unleash the horrors of war, and I was deeply affected. I knew than that it is no longer possible to believe that the future is leading to the best of all possible worlds. My generation is searching for ways to replace the loss of the certainty that was enjoyed by your generation and which formed my view of the world while growing up."

"It is ironic that learning how to ride, the very thing I avoided as a child, has become the centerpiece of my life at Los Olivares. Luis Eduardo made clear that riding a horse on a Spanish farm is an important skill. So he got proper riding clothes for Manuel and me and we take riding lessons every morning before breakfast from Beltran, the farm manager. I completely trusted that he would make me into a proper Spanish equestrian. And he did. Even Begonia, Luis Eduardo's stepmother, says so." My father was listening intensely, so I dared to continue.

"Becoming friends with Guillermo and so easily crossing class boundaries gave me the courage to express myself more forcefully. Being around the lively, interesting people here has helped me feel things I never felt before, which I have come to see as a valuable thing. Little by little, I am being transformed into something resembling a distinct personality, at least in comparison to the cautious young man I was when I arrived. I have begun to realize that my shyness was a way of avoiding disagreements that might lead to confrontations."

"My friendships with Guillermo and Manuel are not like those shared by my three Dublin friends. They and I are from the same sort of families and shared traditions. But my friendship here with Guillermo and Manuel is with people who are fundamentally different from each other, and we knew that there were long odds that we ever become friends. I do not want to be cut off from the mutual trust and support of my friends here. I am not the person I was when I left London, and have no desire to return to that way of life."

I stopped at this point, relieved to have been so straightforward with my father. But from the anxious look on his face, he didn't seem so sure he liked what he was hearing.

We looked at each other in silence for a long time before he said, "Well, Edwin, you seem to have become very self-aware. What you say is interesting, and I am glad for your frankness, but I am not convinced that you can sustain the changes you talk about. We are who we are, dear boy. Do be your old sensible self and come home with me to Dublin. I cannot manage the family business forever, and you will need time to prepare to take over. I have to leave here soon but will give you money to come to Dublin as soon as you are well enough to travel."

I had given this possibility a great deal of thought, and knew that I could not accept his offer. I realized he and I were strangers, and that he had no idea how to change that.

"I like what I find here; straightforwardness, emotional expressiveness, and a certain casualness, not to say a charming silliness sometimes, as well as great seriousness about what is happening politically. I intend to stay here for the immediate and probably the indefinite future."

"That's balderdash, Edwin. You have never disagreed with my advice and are not in a fit state to do so now. You are much too young to be making decisions about your place in the world. I would never hire a manager in my company unless he is over 40, and until that age, one's opinions are not reliable. You are a mere boy and cannot have the wisdom to reinvent your life. And, by the way, how will you support yourself?

The money your dear mother left you will not last long. You cannot be a children's tutor forever."

"I intend to become a journalist and write about the Spain that I have come to know and admire, to counter the snobbish way that this country is described in Baedeker's and the British newspapers."

"Journalism! Good heavens, what next! That's not a profession so much as a way to profit from gossip."

"Be that as it may, the world is getting smaller, and it is past time to find ways to learn about the world honestly and without preconceptions or bias. Straight-forward journalism is the only way people will know about the world."

At that, I felt an enormous tiredness coming over me. I was overwhelmed but exhilarated, having been able to so directly express myself to Papa, from my heart. I was grateful that he had listened to me. It was the first time I was able to express opinions that I knew he did not share and that probably neither of us understood. Little by little I was being transformed into something resembling an independent person, at least compared with the cautious young man I was when I came to Spain.

The next morning I woke up with a sense of self-confidence I had not felt before. Yes, I would stay here, and yes, I would try my best to become a journalist.

Eventually, Papa came to my room and sat down quietly so as not to disturb me. Katherine and Luis Eduardo followed him and said, "Sorry to intrude, but it is such a lovely day and we wondered if Edwin is up to going outside for some fresh air."

"What do think, Edwin?" Papa asked.

"It is, indeed, a lovely day, and I am feeling much better. Perhaps we could take a walk around Los Olivares. I especially want to go to the stables to see my horse and to show Papa the repaired and repainted schoolhouse."

Luis Eduardo said, "There is a wheelchair in the next room, and I can arrange for Beltran to push it." Luis Eduardo assured Consolata that they would walk carefully and stop when I get tired. He sent for Beltran, who pushed me in the wheelchair through the house.

I was exhilarated at being in the open air and chatted about what we were seeing. Light filtered through poplar trees, dappling the ground and the blooming azalea bushes.

I pointed out Katherine's studio building and the schoolhouse at the end of the driveway. When we got to the stable, horses were poking their heads out of their stalls. I stopped in front of a dappled white horse that whinnied happily at the sight of me. "This is my horse, Maxim." The horse lowered his head in greeting me, and I enthusiastically stroked his face and shoulders, saying, "I am so happy to see you and tell you that I shall soon be able for the two of us to ride together." I was thrilled to be with my horse, and the little party stopped at the stables for a few minutes. Papa seemed enthralled, which pleased me very much.

I felt that I was fading and asked to be taken back to my room, saying that we could postpone the visit to the school house for another day. Consolata met us at the front door and with Beltran took me to my room and settled me in bed. Katherine gave me a mid-day dose of morphine. As I lay in bed, sounds from the *Misiones Pedagogicas* drifted through the open window. I could hear the distant choral singing, along with people talking loudly in outdoor meetings that I presumed were about politics in the New Spain. I was content, happy even, falling into a peaceful sleep.

Later that day Papa was in my room when Katherine said that the children wanted to visit me and were waiting outside. My heart lifted at the prospect. I asked Papa to put pillows behind my back and help me sit up, comb my hair, and spritz scent on my bedclothes.

Leander, Oscar, and Ottilie entered shyly, beautiful in their best clothes, the parts in their hair straight, their hands and faces clean, wearing their best shoes. We looked at each other solemnly for a few minutes, and then Leander took the hands of his brother and sister and led them close to my bed. He said, "We are very sad that you were hurt, and we pray for you every day."

I was overwhelmed by their presence and the sadness in their eyes. I burst into tears, and so did they. Katherine gave handkerchiefs to the children and to me. One by one I took their hands in mine and thanked them for coming. We stayed quietly together, looking at each other. Then Ottilie took from her pocked a smooth stone onto which my name and theirs were painted. She said, "We want you to keep this always. We think it will bring you good luck and Consolata agrees. The stones you gave us when you arrived are the best gift we ever got, and we want to give you one, too." I took the stone and laid it on my chest. "I will keep it here near my heart and will never forget you."

Katherine signaled that it was time to leave. I shook the boys' hands and hugged Ottilie, and they were ushered to the door. As they left, I called out cheerfully,' "Don't forget to study your English verbs." They giggled and closed the door.

Papa beamed. "Goodness gracious me, Edwin, what a following you have here. Those beautiful children obviously love you." Then he kissed me on the forehead and left.

A while later Manuel came to visit. I was very glad to see him and asked about *Misiones Pedagogicas*. He sat in armchair next to me and said that it seemed like most of the villagers were participating in its activities, visiting the exhibition of paintings, and were especially interested in the portraits of the local families.

People were slowly joining the chorus. It was especially popular and there were practices every day before lunch. They are enthusiastic participants who continue singing all day after practice.

Every evening a different play was performed on the makeshift stage in front of the village hall, which drew most of the inhabitants of the village. "They are bedazzled by the sets and costumes," he said, "and are attentive to the elaborate speeches made by the actors. They especially love Romeo and Juliet, weeping and hugging each other at the end when both characters die and the final sad words are spoken:

> "A glooming peace this morning with it brings;
> the sun, for sorrow, will not show his head.
> For never was a story of more woe
> than this of Juliet and her Romeo."

A few of the villagers helping set up the library were chosen because they could read a little, and were being trained to manage and keep track of the books and other materials such as maps, recordings and the wind-up record player, and the radio.

Another group was learning how to maintain the gasoline generator that produced electricity, which they thought of as a kind of magic, and how to run the wires taking this new phenomenon to the town hall, the church and parsonage, the barracks of the Civil Guard, and the schoolhouse.

At the end of the day, big dinners were served in the principal plaza. Luis Eduardo, Katherine and their children strolled from table to table greeting everyone with handshakes. Villagers talked with Luis Eduardo and his family as though they had known each other for a long time. Contacts were being established across a cultural gap of thousands of years.

This breaking down of barriers between people surprised everybody, generating a kind of palpable "generosity of spirit."

Here were descendants of people who had conquered America and had risen against Napoleon's attempts to conquer Spain. Here was the untapped undirected energy of Spain, the human group that had never been assimilated in to the life in modern times. Although contact between illiterate peasants and middle class university students would not lead to concrete achievements, interactions of tremendous sentimental importance were being established. *Misiones Pedagogicas* students came face to face with the poverty, ignorance, fear, and the dignity of the Spanish Pueblo.

I was grateful to Manuel for his descriptions and impressed by his enthusiasm for the way *Misiones Pedagogicas* was being received by the villagers.

"Has opposition developed?" I asked.

"There are holdouts of course, older people who are suspicious and without the slightest idea of what to make of all this commotion. They sit together on the black benches in the plaza, arms folded, stern looks on their faces. They have never seen anything like *Misiones Pedagogicas*, and don't want to have anything to do with it. Their priest tells them not to participate, and so they don't. He has nothing good to say about these goings on."

Nonetheless, both of us were amazed by what was taking place. I was puzzled about how such a program of education had come into being in such an early stage of the new Republican government.

I asked Manuel if he knew about the origins of *Misiones Pedagogicas*. He said that he happened to know quite a lot about it because the idea of sharing cultural resources with all of Spain was one of the basic principles of the *Institution Libre*, the educational system where he had been educated.

At Manuel's suggestion, I decided to join the discussions about Spanish political history, which were taking place every morning at nine am, led by Horatio de Calderone, a young lecturer in Spanish history from the University of Madrid.

The next morning Sr. de Calderone came to see me in my makeshift bedroom. He said that his group was being introduced to the concept of political inclusion and participation in political life, starting with explanations about what voting was and was not. For many of the participants voting was a great mystery. They had to sign or make their mark on a piece of paper, which made them suspicious. What did they get for that and why must people vote, anyway? Everyone was dimly aware of "Madrid" but believed that it was best to stay away from anything that was from there, as though it was a disease - until *Misiones Pedagogicas* arrived, that is.

For what to them must have seemed like the first time, people from the village were experiencing something good that came from Madrid. They were confused by that, and skeptical about whether there was some kind of secret agenda. Sr. de Calderone explained to the group that the election of the new Republican government led directly to their decision to establish *Misiones Pedagogicas*, which, in turn, led to the experiences they were having.

None of this made much sense to a group of people who never had control over their lives, and who had to beg or steal whatever they could to make their meager lives bearable. Nothing had ever come easily and it was hard to believe that *Misiones Pedagogicas* was an unencumbered "gift." For some villagers the sense of wonder took a more skeptical form. Were these visitors not tax collectors? Not agents looking for cheap land, or coming to draft soldiers? Slowly the villagers realized that the strangers had come to give something to the village: books, medicines, pictures, respect.

Sr. de Calderone said that at the group's second meeting someone shouted from the crowd, "What does Beltran think? We trust him."

Sr. de Calderone decided to talk with Beltran about his possible participation in the political discussions. Beltran was clearly pleased to be described this way, and said, "I have not seen myself this way but I suppose others do. If you think it would be helpful I can join the discussions."

Beltran and Sr. de Calderone talked about how to make the local people understand that their vote was essential to their future, because voting was the only way a government could know what the country wanted. Beltran came up with the idea that we needed to find examples of how voting could lead to change that benefitted the villagers. Apart from *Misiones Pedagogicas*, there had been nothing to speak of from the central governments in Madrid. But there was a long list of things that needed to change, and a long tragic history of failed attempts to do so.

Beltran said that peasants knew about the tradition in Andalusia of *caciqueismo,* a long standing system of manipulation of elections that allowed a small group of entrenched leaders to retain indefinite political control. After a local election, there was an automatic "change of government" from one established political party to another, like clockwork. This cycle of declaring political "winners" and "losers" was unrelated to actual votes. This regular reallocation of political power meant a complete change of functionaries, creating unemployment, administrative chaos, and a culture of bribes. The Republican government had quickly made regulations to control these corrupt voting processes. In addition the government established voting rights for women. Now that all Spaniards had the right to vote, they had to do so because there was no other way for their voices to be heard.

Beltran said that this sort of rambling explanation would not be easily understood by skeptical villagers, and that they needed to be reminded that the village had received two special benefits: the school founded by Dona Luisa many years ago, and more recently led by Katherine and her project to build new cottages for their workers, which they would occupy rent-free.

Beltran was energized by the opportunity to help people understand their need to change their attitudes toward their own futures. He was clearly pleased to be included and thanked them for including him in the discussions, shook hands, and left.

This was a long, but interesting explanation for me to listen to, but I was growing fatigued. Manuel noticed my restlessness, and made a proposal: "Would you like to be taken to the village to participate in some of the *Misiones Pedagogicas* activities? Everyone knows that you were shot during the demonstration against the Civil Guard."

Just at that moment, Consolata came in and heard us talking about visiting the village. "But Edwin, you have only been back from the hospital for a few days," she said apprehensively, "Perhaps going to the village is asking too much."

"*Misiones Pedagogicas* will be leaving soon, and I want to participate."

Consolata went to fetch Katherine. Manuel and I looked at each other, silently vowing to overcome whatever opposition there would be to my visiting the village. Katherine came in with Consolata, Luis Eduardo, and my father, all of them looking serious.

"What have the two of you been up to?"

"Just thinking about a visit to the village while *Misiones Pedagogicas* is here," I said, sitting straight up in my bed, smiling. Luis Eduardo asked Papa what he thought.

"Look here, if Edwin thinks he is up to visit, I think we should find a way to do that."

I grinned from ear-to-ear at my father's comment.

Luis Eduardo frowned slightly. "Let me see if you can walk across the room with my help."

I dropped my legs off the side of the bed. "But first, I want to see if I can stand up by myself." I sat for a few minutes, gathering strength and abruptly stood. Standing was a little wobbly, but I deflected help and stood erect for a few minutes. I clutched Luis Eduardo's arm, my legs shaking, and took a step. I stood still for a few seconds, wincing in pain, took another step, stood for several minutes by myself looking intently at my father before stepping backward and sat down on the bed. Then, almost immediately, I stood up, flashing a smile.

Luis Eduardo clapped me on the back saying, "Well done!"

I sank back onto the pillows. I began thinking that a visit to *Misiones Pedagogicas* and the schoolhouse would let my father see for himself how much his son was connected to local life, and how invigorating that was for me.

Luis Eduardo said, "I think the best way to get Edwin to the village is to drive him in my car. He could sit in the back seat with pillows propping him up, and a blanket to keep him warm if it gets chilly. The road is full of potholes so I will drive slowly and it should only take ten minutes."

My eyes glowed at the prospect. "Can we have Guillermo and Manuel in the car? They could sit in the back with me, with Papa in front next to Luis Eduardo." Then I said firmly, "When we get to the village, I want to walk from the car. Manuel and Guillermo can support me, and we can bring the wheelchair in the car in case it is needed."

My father smiled indulgently, Consolata frowned and crossed herself as Katharine looked at me with admiration.

The next morning Luis Eduardo brought his car to the front of the house. I got into the back with Guillermo and Manuel, my father in front with Luis Eduardo. We drove slowly down the driveway and into the village. I felt tremendously empowered by our little adventure. Manuel and Guillermo and were also excited to be visiting *Misiones Pedagogicas* with all me. When we got to the village, we drove to the Town Hall where the paintings had been hung. The visitors from *Misiones Pedagogicas* and a crowd of villagers stared at us.

Everyone was quiet as I got out of the car, at which point the crowd applauded energetically, and a bunch of wildflowers was presented to me. I thanked the group for their welcome and walked up the steps to the porch, with Manuel and Guillermo's help, then sat down on the wheelchair and was rolled into the Town Hall to look at the paintings. Inside there was a group of children in a room listening to an explanation of one the paintings by a *Misiones Pedagogicas* visitor. He was pointing out the life-sized equestrian portrait of Philip II.

They stood aside as we entered. I shook each of their hands, telling them how lucky they were to be able to see these magnificent paintings because the only other place to see them was in a museum in Madrid.

"But what is Madrid?" asked a little girl at the back of the group. I replied that it was a big city in the center of Spain, far away from their village.

"But what is a city?" someone else asked.

"It is a place where many, many people live, and where the government decides to do the things that will make Spain a great country."

Another girl asked. "But what is a country?"

"Spain is a country, like other countries, such as England, where I come from. In Spain, people talk Spanish. In England, people talk English. People in one country are different from other countries, but they share many things, too. We are all people, each country learns from the other."

"I am impressed by the questions you have asked," I said. "You are learning things that will be useful to you as you grow older. Thank you for being here and being so interested in these great paintings."

One boy said eagerly, "The people in the pictures look so real we thought they would jump from the wall into the room where we are standing." We were touched by the boy's comment, fully aware that he had understood what a painting was and what it was not.

"Well," I said, "these portraits were made years ago, and none of them has left their frames yet." The children giggled again.

Papa was especially enthusiastic, and said to no one in particular "Well done!" I stood up again and went to the building's porch.

A group of peasants came up to us, staring at us and one of the girls said,

"We know that you are Don Edwin, sir, and that you were part of our fight against the Civil Guard. We want to thank you for that, and pray for you to get better soon." Then they broke into applause.

All of this inspired me. There was an awkward silence until Luis Eduardo announced, "Thank you all for looking at these paintings. They are some of the most beautiful ever made and are here because the new government in Madrid wants you to be able to see them and hear about their history. You are all Spanish subjects and deserve to share the things that have made Spain great."

The children smiled from ear-to-ear, not so much because of what Luis Eduardo said but because they were in the same room as he, a person whom they had heard about all their lives but never seen. Everyone savored this moment.

I looked at our little group to see if they were as awed as I was by the questions from these children.

My father turned to me and whispered, "Edwin, how are you holding up"?

"I am feeling very strong."

I could see that he was becoming a little overwhelmed by all this affection toward me. I noticed and said, "Papa, the openness that you see toward me is the thing that makes me feel so good about being here. Despite their humiliating servitude, Spanish peasants have not lost their dignity or good Spanish manners or their sense of humor. The differences between ordinary Spaniards and me are genuine but they are not barriers. Their openness is infectious and has helped me become more open myself."

Although we were not in private, I said that "until coming here I never realized the stiffness and formality of our lives in Dublin. I never saw you and my mother, or more or less any of your friends, embrace, or, for that matter, even touch each other beyond walking arm-in-arm occasionally. I only realized how peculiar that was when I saw the interactions between Luis Eduardo and Katharine, who greet each other with kisses and stroll arm-in-arm after dinner. I do not mean to imply that you and my mother did not love each other, only that the physical expression of your affection has always been absent."

I was feeling very emotional at being able to talk to Papa this way, but he was exasperated. "I do not appreciate being lectured about your mother and me. We were happily married for twenty years and always acted in ways that were appropriate for our social position. I dearly loved her and still have not recovered from her death. Does it take a special kind of courage to speak to me?"

"Not about the inconsequentialities of life, no. But talking about things that matter is another story. Then we dry up and change the subject." I took a deep breath, and looked directly at my father. "I want to tell you something that I have never had the courage to say to you, and you have never said to me. "

I paused, waiting somehow for reassurance. He looked at me with the sort of patience that I had never seen in his face before. I took another breath and plunged ahead.

"I feel deep affection for you and hold you very dear. I love you."

We looked at each other for a long time, with affection that I will never forget. Finally, I said that I was becoming tired, and my pain was increasing. "Papa, I have to rest now, but I want to continue our talk tomorrow." My father leaned over and kissed me for the second time I remember, on my forehead. Then he grasped the handles of the wheelchair, but I shook my head and walked with him, arm in arm.

I was very glad to have shared myself and my feelings. It was past time when Papa could tell me what to do, and I was grateful that he listened to me. It was also the first time I expressed opinions that I knew he did not share, and that probably neither of us understood very well.

We left the town hall and moved slowly around the village, passing the choral rehearsal and the construction of the stage in front of the church, and went to look at Katherine's exhibition. I walked up the steps of the house with help from Luis Eduardo and Papa. Guillermo and Manuel held me by my arms as I slowly went inside. Crowds of visitors were in the rooms looking at the pictures of themselves and their neighbors, chatting excitedly among themselves, becoming quiet as we entered. The group stood aside as we walked around the exhibition, staring at us and whispering to each other.

Manuel asked, "Are any of you or your families in these photographs? Can you show us?" There was an immediate stir as people moved to where pictures of them or their families were hung, standing proudly in front of them. Finally, someone said, "Our priest told us that having pictures of ourselves was a sin of vanity. But we are so happy to have our pictures that we just confessed our sin and put them on our walls anyway." The group smiled at that remark and many laughed, obviously glad that someone from the village had the courage to make fun of their priest in front of us.

Luis Eduardo brought the car and we slowly went down the stairs, got into the car, and left to applause and waves of goodbye. When we got to Los Olivares, I was tired but happy. Manuel went to the schoolhouse to make plans for my father's visit there. Papa and I went to the loggia and sat at a little table where Consolata brought tea.

Early the next morning Manuel and the students met at the schoolhouse to prepare for our "official" visit with my father. A banner hung on the front wall of the school that read in English, "Welcome to Our Hero". The students were wearing their new school clothes.

I introduced Papa, who said in his broken Spanish, "Many thanks for your welcome. As you can see, my son is getting better each day, not the least because of the support he gets from you and his friends here. I am grateful to all of you for that."

The students then sang "Rule Britannia" in their rough-and-tumble English to great applause from them and their visitors. The students chattered happily as they devoured the sweet biscuits that Consolata had brought, and served them to the visitors. Manuel gave my father a tour of the restored schoolhouse and the vegetable garden at the back.

Then all the students gathered in front of the schoolhouse for a formal photograph. They brought chairs for Papa, Manuel, and myself and the students assembled in rows behind them. Katherine placed her camera a few feet in front of the schoolhouse on a tripod. Manuel passed around a comb for the students to use to fix their hair. In order to be sure that the students would not move during the photo and he shouted gleefully "Think of your feet as being glued to the ground!" He sat down between my father and me. Katherine began taking photographs. The students tried hard to repress their nervous giggles and after ten minutes all was complete. Katherine promised the students that every household in the village would get a framed copy of the photograph, generating gasps and applause.

It suddenly dawned on her that a photo of my father and me together would be a grand memorial of this visit, and the beginning of our connecting with each other for what seemed to be the first time. Papa sat on a stone wall surrounding the school in his shirt sleeves, without a tie, wearing an elegant straw hat borrowed from Luis Eduardo as protection against the sun. He looked content. I stood next to him with my hand on his shoulder. Katherine paused, then smiled, and said, "The two of you look like father and son."

We stayed a little longer and then walked slowly arm in arm to the main house.

When we got to my room, Papa helped me into bed and sat in a nearby chair. I was tired, but happy that Papa had been able to see something of my life there, and especially to see that I had become so deeply connected with the people who lived there. Ever the Irishman, he ordered tea for both of us, which we drank in peaceful silence.

Finally my father took my hands in his and said quietly, "You spoke to me yesterday not only as my son, but as a young man with his own ideas. It is obvious that being here has been good for you."

I replied, "Dearest Papa, thank you for saying that. I have to say that I am glad that we started to talk about things that are important to both of us."

We sat together for a long time until I quietly said, "I will always be British and am proud of that. But I am determined to learn from experiences in the other parts of the world.

Papa listened carefully and then said gravely, "I can only hope that your interest in Spain does not lead to your joining one side or the other, on an impulse. Being reckless is not the same thing as being brave. You are a wonderful son, and always have been. I love you for that and dare to

148

hope you feel the same toward me. You have all my support in whatever you decide to do in life. If that means accepting you as a journalist, so be it. I will help you with an open heart. "

I was moved to tears and could only say "thank you." I stood up from my bed and we embraced for a long time.

The next day Papa was driven to Granada where he caught the Madrid Express.

During Papa's long journey back to Dublin, he wrote me a letter which included one of A. E. Housman's sentimental poems from a book that had been carried by English soldiers to the trenches in World War I:

> I shall squander life no more
> Days lost, I know not how.
> I shall retrieve them now
> Now I shall keep the vows
> I never kept before.
> Today I shall be strong
> No more shall yield to wrong.

The Cypresses Believe in God by Jose Maria Gironella, 1995. This is a first novel by a Catholic author who attempted to approach the many nuances and subtleties among all the factions on the eve of the Spanish Civil War.

The Doves of War by Paul Preston, 2002. This tells the forgotten war stories of three exceptional women whose lives were starkly altered by the Spanish Civil War, including Mercedes Sanz Bachiller, the most powerful woman in the Francoist zone.

Franco: A Biography by Paul Preston, 1993. Preston has assembled a detailed and very readable story of Generalisimo Franco's life (1892 – 1975).

Frederico Garcia Lorca: A Life by Ian Gibson, 1989. This is the authoritative history of the death of the poet Lorca.

Homage to Catalonia by George Orwell, 1938. This is the best of many books about the Spanish Civil War by a foreigner.

Life and Death of a Spanish Town by Elliot Paul, 1937. This is based on his actual experiences of living in the town of Santa Eulària des Riu on the Spanish island of Ibiza at the outbreak of the Spanish Civil War.

Spain by Jan Morris, 1954. Morris portrays a country on the edge of Europe in the strong grip of State and Church.

The Spanish Civil War by Sir Hugh Thomas, 1961. This stands without rival as the most balanced and comprehensive book on the subject of the Spanish Civil War.

The Spanish Cockpit by Franz Borkenau, 1937. This book has been widely praised and is of exceptional interest to those who want to know what was going on in Spain in 1936.

The Spanish Labyrinth by Gerald Brennan, 1943. This has become the classic account of the background to the Spanish Civil War.